Ironman had had enough

Carl Lyons's pati[...]
he raised his head [...]e
target of enemy fi[...]

The terrorists had [...]
was the time to go [...] Lyons rammed
a twenty-round box of ammo into his Konzak
and stood up.

Two bursts of enemy autofire swept toward him
immediately. The assault shotgun boomed once,
cutting off one sweep of lead before it reached
him.

Oblivious to the danger that awaited him, the
Able Team warrior walked directly toward the
enemy's position. In a daze he sprayed the path
ahead with shotgun fire, no longer aware of the
bullets that cut through the air around him or of
the shouts from his own men.

Gadgets Schwarz watched helplessly as his friend
walked toward certain death. He knew there was
little he could do to protect him.

Carl Lyons had gone mad!

Mack Bolan's

ABLE TEAM

ABLE TEAM

DEATH RIDE

Dick Stivers

A GOLD EAGLE BOOK FROM
W✹RLDWIDE

TORONTO • NEW YORK • LONDON • PARIS
AMSTERDAM • STOCKHOLM • HAMBURG
ATHENS • MILAN • TOKYO • SYDNEY

First edition April 1987

ISBN 0-373-61229-X

Special thanks and acknowledgment to
Tom Arnett for his contribution to this work.

Printed in Canada

PROLOGUE

"Don't kill my mommy. Don't kill my mommy," eight-year-old Andrew repeated over and over.

Lisa Frane scooped up the scrawny boy in her arms, saying, "Hush, now. No one's going to hurt your mother. Everything's okay."

Karen Yates gently took the frightened child from the pale young woman. Instead of cuddling the small boy, she sat him astride her knees facing her in the weak light from the oil lamp.

"Comforting is a good thing," Karen said to Frane, "but try not to suppress fear. Try to bring it out instead."

Karen focused her attention on Andrew and, in a gentle voice, asked, "Who's going to kill your mommy?"

A light breeze filtered through the window screen. It ruffled the boy's shaggy blond hair. It also caused Lisa Frane's shapeless muslin shirt to billow around her narrow shoulders. Outside, the darkness was alive with the drone of insects and the monotonous chirp of tree frogs. The river's constant murmur filled the occasional silence.

Andrew paused for breath and looked directly into Karen's green eyes. She was a small woman in her early thirties, although the boy knew only that she was a figure of authority. Her red hair was cropped in short, tight curls, framing an elfin face.

Andrew sniffed twice, before answering, "Sensei. Sensei leaps on her, and he's going to kill her."

"Sensei's gone away. He'll never come back."

"Where's Mommy? I want Mommy."

"Your mommy's at home in Cleveland, working. She sent Lisa and me to take care of you instead. We'll do the best we can, and you'll be home with your mommy in ten more days. Can you count to ten?"

Andrew nodded.

"Let's count to ten together. Then you go back to sleep until it's light. Okay?"

The nod was even more reluctant, but Andrew counted along and let himself be put in his hammock. He quickly fell asleep.

Karen nodded for Frane to follow her outside into the darkness.

"You did well to get to Andrew and comfort him," she told Frane, "but Pat says never to deny their fears. We've come to help these nine children face their experience. This place represents a terrible period of their lives. Most of their fathers died here. The children were more brainwashed than brought up. So help them talk about it. Don't try to quiet their fears. Get them to express them in words, then we can deal with them."

"So now the Reverend Quincey's 'Pat,' is he?" Frane teased. She stuffed her hands into the pockets of her calf-length full skirt.

Karen smiled in the light of the quarter moon. Briefly she noted Frane's switch from tight to baggy clothes. Then she brought her mind back to the teasing.

"We can't live on a last-name basis forever. You will remember to encourage the children to talk about their anxieties, won't you?"

"Promise. You were here during the massacre, weren't you?"

"Massacre? That's not what I'd call it. But, yes. I was here from almost the beginning, right up to the end," Karen answered, shuddering.

The two American women were silent for a minute, gazing at the small clearing in the middle of the Guyanese rain forest. A caiman splashed as it slid into the river south of the camp. Two fish jumped where the Pomeroon River curved to the north of them.

Only six months ago nearly seventy families had lived there. All had been cult members, followers of Sensei Abraham Lincoln Arnold. Now, the forest had begun to move in, to repossess the land once covered by the buildings that had formed the compound's perimeter.

There had been two wooden barracks. Only one still stood. When their small party, which included one man, three women and nine children, had arrived sixteen days ago, they had moved into it.

"If you were here from the beginning, either you or your husband must have been one of the elders," Frane prompted.

"George was second-in-command."

"And he was murdered when the American troops stormed the place?"

Karen Yates turned her head to look at her companion. "You really don't know what happened, do you? It was my husband who was the murderer. He disappeared. I don't know if he's dead or alive."

"You must hate him to call him a murderer."

Karen shook her head, as if she wanted to wake from a dream. Around them, tropical trees tossed their branches in the gentle wind. The fading moon transformed the motion of the branches into a macabre shadow dance on the small clearing.

"Sensei trained everyone in the martial arts, even the very young children. He trained us in *ninjitsu*, the art of the ninja. Then he started sending some of the men on business trips for the church—Arnold called us the Church of the Rising Sons.''

''It was only much later that we learned the men were members of an assassination squad, that they were flying to the United States to assassinate people those in power here in Guyana didn't like. We also know they did a lot of the government's dirty work within Guyana. It was the price we paid to be left alone. Later, we found out that Sensei was hiring the team out to mercenary units as well, and pocketing the proceeds.''

''That's why the U.S. sent an antiterrorist team here. They were good men. They protected the children, even as they fought their parents.''

Karen let her voice trail off into silence.

Dawn had broken.

A monkey howled in the distance, and a bird began its morning serenade to the camp.

''You don't know your husband was a killer. You only have the Americans' word for it,'' Frane argued.

''One of the assassins talked. When Pat walked in here unarmed, we knew that Sensei would try to kill him. In the end, he tied him to that tree.'' She pointed to one in the center of the compound. ''He was bait to pull the other three in.''

''Three? Against how many did you say?''

''Over fifty Ninja-trained assassins. There were four men including Pat Quincey, but he's deadly when he gets going.''

''You must be joking.''

Karen shook her head and lapsed into silence. She was thinking of Able Team. Especially of Rosario Blancanales, who had protected the children through the heat of the battle.

''Who were the other three—Superman, Captain Marvel and Spiderman?''

"Just men, men who are willing to put their lives on the line to stop people like Sensei and...and my husband. They moved us to a facility near Washington and kept us there while Quincey worked with the children. Most adjusted quickly, except these nine. That's why we brought them back here."

"Tell me more about this group of men."

Karen Yates described the battle briefly, pointing to where things took place. Then she lapsed into silence, remembering.

Frane tried several more times to start the conversation again, but Karen didn't hear her. She finally left the woman to her thoughts.

The bird's serenade ended, but Karen failed to notice.

It was the sound of approaching trucks that jolted her back to awareness. She glanced at her watch. Five-thirty local time. Who'd be approaching the camp at this hour? She looked around. Frane had disappeared. Patrick Quincey, the ex-Green Beret, Episcopalian minister and psychologist who specialized in deprogramming, wasn't up yet. It looked as if it would be up to her to see who was arriving.

The compound was surrounded on three sides by the Pomeroon. The fourth side was partially blocked by a barn, a dilapidated generator shed and a few lengths of rusting barbed-wire fence. It was the dry season, and the coarse grass and weeds inside the enclosed area had been worn into a network of paths.

Karen crossed the compound and stepped through the ruined fence. She could hear several trucks coming toward her in low gear. Saplings and weeds had taken over the trail in the six months since the cult had been wiped out, but with a Jeep and a truck with four-wheel drive Quincey had been able to move them in. She knew that whoever was approaching would have little difficulty in reaching the compound.

Karen stood waiting, speculating on who it could be. The best bet was Guyanese troops. Pat Quincey had cleared this treatment session with the government, had paid the usual bribes and had had little trouble getting permission for a short stay. The government—and its employees—could use all the U.S. dollars it could get.

An army jeep was the first vehicle to appear. Behind it rumbled two brown trucks, the type of vehicles usually used to transport troops.

Karen began to wonder if she should have some support with her before she asked what they wanted. The Guyanese army wasn't known for the respect it showed the civilian population. But it was too late. She'd been spotted, and the jeep sped toward her, coming to a rocking stop just inches short of running her down.

"That's what I call a cool homecoming," a voice from the jeep said. "My lovely wife waiting at the gate to meet me."

"George!" the word exploded from Karen as if she'd been punched in the gut.

"Who was you expectin', little mama? Stevie Wonder?"

The three trucks crept to a halt behind the jeep. George emerged from the front passenger seat of the jeep. He stretched his six-foot frame and ran stubby fingers through his short Afro. Karen knew he was thirty-seven, but the black ninja-trained killer didn't look a day more than twenty-five.

"You're not with the Guyanese army?"

"Course not. I'm with my own army. Does this look like a Guyanese chicken-shit uniform?"

George Yates was wearing black fatigues and a black officer's billed cap. He carried an eighteen-inch-long swagger stick.

While they had been talking, men in black fatigues had piled out of the back of the three trucks. A tall officer climbed out of a truck cab and approached George. The rest of the men milled around. Karen noticed they wore head-bands of black cloth. George snapped out orders to the man wearing the officer's cap.

"Round up everyone in the compound. Don't let the children run into the bush."

The officer looked briefly at Karen, then turned and spoke in a foreign language to his troops, who filed quietly into the compound.

"What are you doing?" Karen demanded. "Who are they? I assumed you were with Guyanese, but these people don't speak English."

"Women shouldn't question their husbands," George replied airily.

"George, Sensei claimed you divorced me. I will not take orders from you."

The fancy swagger stick jabbed forward, catching Karen in the solar plexus. She doubled over, then fell to her knees, gasping and retching as she tried to breathe.

"No more back talk, woman. Do as you're told."

He grabbed Karen by the collar of her shirt and easily hoisted her to her feet. He held her there until she was able to stand on her own.

"Now, where's your room?"

"What's this all about?" Karen demanded.

The stick whistled and struck the side of her thigh. She winced.

"Your room?"

"The children's barracks. The men's was burned."

"I know. Move your stuff to Sensei's office. Move the children and the other women there. The men will use the barracks."

He added emphasis to the order by bruising her other thigh with the stick.

Karen said nothing but slowly pulled her chin up and glared defiantly at her husband.

"Before you get fancy thoughts, you remember the children, little mama. If the women ain't here to take care of them, those Arabs I'm with will kill them for sure."

"And you'd let them?" Her voice showed the contempt she felt for the man she had once loved.

George flashed a hundred-watt grin at her. "Damned right."

Hanging her head, she fell in behind George as they walked in silence to the barracks. Sleepy children were being escorted to the compound by the silent troops.

In her room, Karen thought back to the nightmare she'd faced in the Guyanese rain forest when she and George had moved there with Arnold's cult. Now her husband was back, trying to fill Sensei's shoes. He wanted to manipulate innocent people. He wanted power.

Karen knew that she and the children were in grave danger. There was only one man other than Quincey who could help them, but she had no way of contacting her old friend. Rosario Blancanales and the team he worked with were back in the States.

Her thoughts were interrupted when the door was thrown open. George Yates stood in the doorway, his face flushed with rage.

"The preacher idiot, where the hell is he?"

Karen had no idea. She felt the bottom drop out of her world. And Able Team, twenty-five hundred miles away, had no idea that her life hung from a frayed thread.

1

The sun clawed its way over the horizon, causing long shadows to stalk the Jornada del Muerto.

Rosario ''Politician'' Blancanales kicked sand off the deserted runway as he walked. The air still held the chill of a New Mexican night, and dust particles sparkled in the red rays of the sun.

Although Politician's hair was almost white, his trim body and his deep tan made him look much younger than he actually was. He wore fatigue pants, combat boots and a light gray jacket over a mesh undershirt.

When the sun hit his eyes, he turned back toward the camp, four one-man tents and a common cook-fly where the group could eat without getting sunstroke. Sand, broken only by patches of brown grass and brittle yucca, stretched to the north and south horizons. To the east and west the blinding surface blended into the hazy blue of distant mountains.

It was Politician's turn to cook, and the rest of the camp would soon be ready for their first meal of the day. They were already up and following Lyons on an early morning run. The cook didn't get to go along; it would only delay breakfast.

Blancanales filled a coffeepot from a plastic container, started a small gas stove and heaped coarsely ground coffee into the pot before putting it on a low flame. He lit the second ring of the propane stove and started preparing the meal.

As always, Lyons was the first back. He enjoyed pushing himself to the limit for the last two miles in order to leave everyone behind. The blond warrior came charging over the last dune as if he had exactly two seconds to rescue Bo Derek from a fate worse than death.

He wore a one-piece triathlon suit, the one he'd worn in the Ironman triathlon. His feet churned the sand like a car spinning its wheels. Lyons hadn't shaved for six days, and his pale blue eyes blazed like two flames in desert scrub.

Blancanales stroked his own three days of growth, then went to a gas-powered refrigerator and pulled out four steaks. When he checked the coffeepot, it was just beginning to bubble. He moved it farther from the heat.

Lyons grabbed a bottle of Gatorade from the table. He was still breathing heavily. Blancanales was wearing a jacket against the desert chill, but Ironman, clad only in the one-piece suit, was perspiring heavily.

"You'd better put on something warmer than that, don't you think?" Politician said.

Lyons looked surprised that someone would question his judgment, in spite of the fact he'd been told the same thing every day since the group had arrived at the deserted air base. He flipped off the bottle cap with his thumb and strode toward his tent.

The other two jogged in together, a small woman and a man. They had covered the last two miles in something under ten minutes.

Hermann Schwarz was better known as Gadgets to the other members of Able Team. He was the same height as Blancanales and just a few pounds lighter. His brown hair covered most of his ears, and he sported a thick mustache. His eyes always twinkled with a sly humor. Gadgets wore blue sweats, which showed heavy salt stains. He ran at an easy stride.

Lao Ti ran right beside him. A lifetime of martial arts training had given her a well-toned and muscular physique. Lao was of Mongolian and Vietnamese descent. Her straight black hair was cropped at the neck. She ran in a lightweight black sweat suit.

When Lao and Gadgets reached the camp, they went their separate ways to change their clothing. As they disappeared, Lyons returned to the cooking area. He was wearing jeans, a plaid shirt and combat boots and was draining the last drops from his bottle of Gatorade.

"What's for breakfast?" he asked.

"The same thing you had yesterday, the morning before that and each morning since we've been here," Politician answered. "Some sort of cereal mix for you, then steak and eggs for everybody."

"What's wrong with that?"

"Steak and eggs used to be a treat. We've got to go to town today. The water reservoir's almost dry. When I get into town, I'm buying something different for breakfast."

"You buy something different and you cook," Lyons answered.

Blancanales sighed.

Lyons cocked his head to one side. "What's that?"

Blancanales stopped pouring boiling water over Lyons's cereal mixture and listened.

"Twin-engine jet. Low."

Lao and Gadgets ran up to join their two colleagues. Gadgets had changed into a safari suit, and Lao wore jeans and a plaid shirt. Neither had taken time to lace their boots.

Lyons was the first to spot the plane. It was mat black. The twin engines attached to the body behind the wings were nearly half the length of the plane.

"It's from Stony Man. Mark the field," Lyons ordered.

He led the charge to the deserted runway that was almost covered by a layer of sand. It ran from northeast to southwest in order to make the most of the prevailing wind. Politician quickly stowed the food in the small refrigerator, away from the sand that the plane would whip up. Then he grabbed a couple of brightly striped hand towels and followed the other three.

Lyons and Gadgets reached the far end of the runway, stripped off their shirts and waved them. Lao pointed her plaid-covered arm into the wind. Politician took his place at the near end of the runway with a towel in each hand.

The base had been built as part of the government plan to keep its defensive air power undercover during the war. It had been abandoned in the late fifties, and the runway hadn't been used or maintained since that time. The sand covered the tarmac in ripples. The runway might be long enough in theory, but the sand would extend the stopping distance by fifty percent.

The black plane came in low from the northeast, but the flaps weren't down.

"Hit the deck," Lyons yelled.

All four members of Able Team sprawled flat as the Sabreliner powered over the runway, its backwash creating a sandstorm.

"Hell!" Gadgets said as he sprang to his feet spitting sand. "He wasn't more than twenty feet off the deck."

The plane circled and came in once more. Able Team quickly resumed their places, but this time the flaps and landing gear were down.

The plane touched, bounced once and held to the sand-covered runway. The pilot put on full reverse thrust as soon as he was sure he was down. Politician stayed at the end of the runway, waving the colored towels to mark the place where it dropped off to sand.

The plane swerved in the loose sand. The pilot applied his wheel brakes unevenly, a tricky piece of work in a plane that had touched down at better than a hundred miles an hour.

The battle for control increased as the plane moved down the field. It swung from one side of the runway to the other in wider and wider arcs. Within inches of the end of the runway, it slid to a full stop.

Able Team ran toward the Sabreliner. The door opened, and Hal Brognola, the Fed in charge of Stony Man operations, leaped to the ground.

Brognola was a heavyset man with gray in his hair and eyes that were hard as flint. He put up with the antics of the men under him, but left little doubt as to who was in charge. Even at that hour of the morning, he was shaved, his gray suit was pressed and his cigar was already half chewed away.

"Tell Grimaldi he did a good job," Gadgets said over the dying scream of the Pratt and Whitney engines.

"How do you know Grimaldi's flapping this bird?" the Fed asked.

Gadgets shrugged. "Who else is that nuts?"

"I heard that. You walk back," came a voice from the door of the plane.

Compared to the other Stony Man warriors, Jack Grimaldi was a small man. His black curly hair was cropped close to his head, and his heavy eyebrows spoke volumes by being raised or lowered over his dark, glittering eyes.

If it flew, Grimaldi could coax more life out of a plane than anyone else. He moved with a confidence and certainty that came from being a master of his craft, a pilot's pilot. Grimaldi jumped down and joined the group.

"Round up your gear," Brognola announced. "We've got a hostage situation in Texas. Just across the state boundary in a small town called Van Horn. You're close, so you're on."

"You mean it's lasted long enough for you to fly all the way from Washington, and we're the only people available?" Lyons growled.

"Not that simple. There have been a couple of political assassinations that may be connected. I was in Phoenix on business. The request for federal help was placed an hour ago. Let's move. You'll get the rest of the briefing on the plane. I'll get a team in here to pick up the rest of your equipment."

"Don't bother," Lyons shouted over his shoulder as he followed the group toward the tents. "We'll be back."

Ten minutes later the black Sabreliner taxied away from the camp. Grimaldi turned it into the wind and increased speed in preparation for the takeoff.

The Able Team warriors changed into Kevlar flak jackets that were equipped with snap pockets for trauma plates. The jackets were lined with a material developed by NASA through which water circulated in microtubing. Chemical packs could heat or cool the bulletproof underwear.

Able Team strapped themselves into seats around the small conference table as the jet thundered over the sand-covered runway, fighting for sufficient speed to reach the sky.

"If this were some other pilot, I'd be shitting bricks," Gadgets confessed. "Now, what's up?"

"In two different cities, people who've fled from Libya have been assassinated—three in one city, two in another. There are three men cornered in a restaurant that belongs to an ex-minister in Khaddafi's government. I can only hope that it's just a coincidence."

"So the Libyan has finally managed to get an assassination team into the U.S. He's been threatening to do that for years," Lyons rumbled. "How many details do you know?"

"Only history. Justice Department helped the Libyan defector change his name and disappear into a small town near the Mexican border. His Spanish is good, and we thought he was safely tucked away.''

"The leak in Washington again!" Lyons exclaimed. "Whoever it is will eventually succeed in setting us up so we don't come back. Are you no closer to getting the bastard?"

Brognola shook his head.

The Sabreliner had leveled out. Lyons unfastened his seat belt, pivoted his chair from the table and stood up.

"I'm going to get the latest from the Van Horn police," Lyons said as he walked to the cockpit.

PATRICK HENRY QUINCEY had awakened early. It was a habit with him. He knew that Karen Yates and Lisa Frane had had a busy night with the children. It was a good sign; it meant the children's fears were beginning to surface. When they admitted their fears, he could deal with them. He felt no charity toward those who had abused the minds of the children to the extent that they were afraid of their own feelings.

The thought of the Church of the Rising Sons and their ninja-trained killers produced a surge of adrenaline. Quincey knew he'd do no more sleeping that morning. He threw his legs over the side of his hammock and sat up, still thinking about killers who had abused their own kids. His thoughts were interrupted by the sound of approaching trucks.

Quincey's Vietnam training propelled him into action. He threw on a shirt, jeans and boots, then slipped out of the barracks to see who was arriving so shortly after dawn.

He slipped out the door and went around the far side of the building. Keeping a barn between himself and the gate, he circled into the forest.

Quincey told himself he was playing silly games, but he continued to listen to his battle instincts. He moved carefully, silently, through the forest, using the skills he had learned in the do-or-die school of Vietnam. The vet came up behind the army vehicles and froze. Men in black fatigues were unloading the trucks. They moved with an easy grace that told of intensive training.

Quincey faded into the woods. He'd stay clear of the camp for a while. He was unarmed and could do little to stop a troop of trained fighters. If their visit was innocent, his absence would do no harm. If it wasn't, Quincey preferred to be free to do what he could to protect the children.

He moved in a cautious arc toward the river. He waded in, but just as he began to swim toward the other bank, he heard the shouting. His absence had been noticed already.

"I DON'T KNOW where he is," Karen told George Yates.

Her simple, unhysterical denial carried a persuasive force that reached even the terrorist leader.

"You must have some idea what he does in the mornings. Where do we look?"

Karen shrugged. "The closest coffeepot. He can't function until he has a couple of coffees."

"Don't play cute, woman. He didn't go to the nearest Howard Johnson's. Where the hell is he?"

She began throwing her possessions into a suitcase. "We leave the coffeepot in the large room downstairs. If he isn't there, he's using the latrine down by the river. The one near the road is for the women."

"Search them both," George Yates said, turning toward the terrorist leader.

"What are you going to do with him?" Karen asked quietly.

George shrugged. "Preachers are usually soft. We need a boy to fetch and carry."

Karen managed to contain her smile. If they were looking for someone soft, Patrick Henry Quincey was definitely the wrong man, but she felt no compulsion to tell that to George.

What she did feel was a sense of being abandoned. She had assumed Quincey would be a source of strength in a time of crisis. Instead, he was absent. Totally absent. She felt he had let her and the children down.

"I'm packed," she told her estranged husband.

"Come on. Soon as you get in the other building, we'll bring over the rest of the women and the brats. You explain the facts of life to them. They get out of line, they're dead. No warnings."

"How can you be so cruel?"

He ignored her. Leading the way out of the barracks, he left her to carry her own suitcases.

The terrorists were still holding Mrs. Johnson and the nine children in the clearing.

"Where's Lisa?" Karen demanded.

"Already in the office building unpacking. Hustle your ass and do the same thing."

"What about Norma Johnson and the children?"

He swung around to look at her. "They're your responsibility. Like I said, if everyone behaves, nothing happens to the kids. You get out of hand, you lose a little girl. You got that?"

Karen remained silent as she looked around the compound.

Most of the terrorists were searching the area. But six of the men were unpacking crates and stringing wire to the roof of the barracks.

"What are they doing?" she asked.

"Putting in our communications," George gloated. "This is going to be a big operation."

Karen nodded. Where the hell was Quincey? she wondered. He'd know how to use the radio, once it was installed. Had he simply run?

George shoved her into the Quonset hut that used to be the camp's office and supply center.

"Get organized," he ordered. "In five minutes you're going to have those kids. You want to see them live, you explain the rules."

As Karen stumbled into the hut, propelled by George's shove, Lisa Frane looked up from where she was sitting in a corner of the office. Two desks and several chairs remained from Sensei's regime, but Frane was sitting on one of her suitcases.

"What's going on?" she asked, trembling.

"My ex-husband is back with a group of foreign mercenaries. I don't know what he's up to, but it isn't good. If we don't do everything we're told, they will rape one of the children."

Frane's face grew even paler. "They wouldn't really. They're just saying that to scare us."

Karen walked to Frane and grabbed her by the shoulders, her fingers digging in painfully. "I know George. He'll do exactly what he says."

Before Frane could answer, the door was thrown open. Two of George's men entered, carrying Norma Johnson's clothing and personal possessions. They dumped the stuff in a heap on the dirty floor and walked out without saying a word.

A moment later, the frightened woman herself was pushed into the Quonset hut. She stumbled and fell onto the pile of clothing. Karen forgot Lisa Frane and went to help the older woman up.

Norma Johnson was forty-two, but she looked much older. Her blond hair was worn in a mass of uncombed curls, but the youthful haircut only accentuated her age. She was a tall, matronly woman with watery blue eyes. Her daughter, Lori, was one of the children Quincey was treating.

"What's happening? Who are these people?"

"They're hired killers," Karen explained. "We mustn't anger them until we can figure a way out of this mess."

"There is no way out," Frane said.

"If I can get a message out, there is. We mustn't lose hope."

Her words seemed to pick up Johnson's spirit. Frane smiled cynically. Karen was about to add something when George herded the children into the Quonset hut.

"You two," he said, looking at Frane and Johnson, "go and get the children's stuff."

He didn't have to say it twice. When the women had gone, he turned to Karen. "We haven't found that bloody preacher yet. Where is he?"

For the first time, Karen had an uneasy feeling that something might have happened to Quincey.

"I told you. I don't know."

"Where's he go in the mornings?"

"He never goes anywhere. What did your butchers do to him?"

"Nothing. If they'd found him, they wouldn't still be looking. When we find him—"

George didn't get to finish. He was interrupted by the arrival of the tall man wearing the officer's cap, the one Karen had seen at the gate.

"We have the wireless connected. Georgetown has been trying to reach you," the tall man reported in flawless English.

"Be right there. Have they found the damn preacher yet?"

"There's no sign of him."

"Strange."

The officer glanced at Karen. "Yes. Very strange."

George misread the meaning of his glance.

"My wife doesn't seem to like the idea. She's probably fallen for the wimp with the collar.

"Karen, this is Captain Mustafa al-Mugarieff. He's in charge of Colonel Khaddafi's freedom brigade."

"Libyans? Here?"

It was the captain who answered, "Colonel Khaddafi is a friend to those who no longer have friends."

"Maybe that's why they no longer have friends," Karen answered.

George slapped her on the cheek, sending her spinning across the room.

"If you wish to live, you'll learn respect," he told her as he followed Mugarieff out of the Quonset hut.

Karen pulled herself to her feet and moved to the dirty window. She followed the progress of her husband and the Libyan commander across the compound. The radio was working. How was she going to get a message out?

Her thoughts were interrupted by the crying of one of the children. Soon she was too immersed in their needs to think of the radio. The other two women returned with the children's possessions. The problem of organizing the small hut for three women and nine children occupied the next two hours.

They were allowed to take the children to the latrines. Food finally arrived at ten o'clock—a yogurt-fruit puree that was too acidic to eat. The children grew restless and irritable in the confined space. Norma Johnson's indignation began to build. Karen could see an explosion coming. How was she going to head it off before it cost a child's life?

Karen knew it was up to her to reach the radio. Quincey had run for it, and the other women still hadn't grasped the seriousness of the situation.

She knew the lives of the nine children depended on her. George wouldn't hesitate to kill a child to keep them in line. He didn't dare back down on his threats. But if she didn't try, the results would be worse over a period of captivity. She had to do something!

At eleven George ordered Karen from the hut.

"I have to leave for a few hours," he told her.

"Still working as a mercenary for the Guyanese government? But that's how you get refuge in this country, isn't it?"

"Shut your mouth and listen, woman. Al-Mugarieff's in charge. My threats haven't been idle ones. Got that?"

She nodded, holding in both her anger and her hope.

"You can take the kids out into the clearing, but no farther."

She nodded again.

"Mugarieff is giving his men English lessons. Help him. Not all the Libyans speak good English."

Karen knew she couldn't look too compliant. "Up yours," she told George.

"You'll come around damn fast."

George turned and marched toward a waiting transport truck. Karen watched six men climb into the back. The rest of the soldiers gathered around to pat them on the back and shout encouragement in their own language.

Karen didn't go back inside the hut, but moved toward the barracks. It was easy to tell which was the radio room; the wire leading to the antenna passed out through the screen.

George climbed into the truck cab beside the driver and saluted his men. Karen took that opportunity to enter the barracks.

There was no one in the hall and she quickly made her way to the door of the radio room. There was no answer when she knocked. Karen tried the knob. The door wasn't locked!

Karen slipped inside and shut the door behind her.

"I thought you'd try this," a cultured voice said. Mugarieff pointed a huge automatic at her. "Now for the consequences." His grin told her that he intended to enjoy whatever was going to happen next.

2

"Are you going to shoot?" Karen questioned.

"You know the rules," the Libyan terrorist told her. "Nothing happens to you. Every time an adult steps out of line, a child pays."

Karen paled but stood firm. It took all of her resolve not to let her panic show. "They pay either way. By the time George has finished brainwashing them, they'll no longer be human."

Mugarieff grinned again. "I will do whatever I must to serve the jihad. Allah's will be done."

"And Allah wants you to become a murderer of women and children?"

"That is enough. I will give you a chance to buy back the child you condemned to an unpleasant death."

Karen raised an eyebrow and waited, not daring to hope. She hated herself for having risked the life of a child, but she'd followed her best judgment at the time. She'd underestimated Mugarieff, but there was nothing she could do about that now.

"There's a tree in the center of the compound. I will tie you to that without a gag. You'll stay there until your servant of the false prophet tries to rescue you. If you try to warn him, the child meets the fate you sentenced her to. If we catch your parson, we release you and the children are left alone. Until another adult steps out of bounds, that is.'

"Trade the child's life for Pat's."

"Not necessarily. I'd prefer to take him alive, but if I can't, we'll shoot him."

There was an oppressive silence in the small room while Karen considered her options. She stared at the rough board walls. Did she have the right to trade one life for another? She knew she couldn't tell the tall, smiling Muslim to let his men gang-rape a child. Slowly she nodded.

PAT QUINCEY was running, but he didn't know what he was running from. His battle instincts had taken him through the jungles of Vietnam. He trusted them. He knew that he had to stay out of reach until he knew who the enemy was and what their plans were.

He kept cutting back from the river and reemerging silently to observe the camp from a new angle. He watched the mercs search for him, but for some reason, they didn't cross the river.

The fate of the three women and nine children worried him. He had watched as they had been moved from the barracks. He was also sure that the cases moved from the trucks to the two-storey wooden building contained weapons, ammunition, food and communications gear.

Lisa Frane had been the first woman to move into the Quonset hut. Quincey thought something just wasn't right. She must have been packed before the trucks even arrived to have made the move so quickly. But he also knew that Lisa had few belongings and probably kept things in her suitcase.

His suspicions returned later when he saw the leader, a tall man, stop Frane and have a lengthy discussion with her. But the frightened look on Frane's face dispelled any misgivings that he had.

The children weren't being treated cruelly, and Quincey decided he could therefore stay hidden for a while longer. He thought of heading for Georgetown and discarded the idea.

The troops had moved too openly, too blatantly. He wasn't going to get help from the Guyanese government. He knew his own government well enough to know that the U.S. couldn't act in time. It would be up to him.

The hot sun and his parched throat told him that he needed liquid. He could skip food if he had to, but he'd be useless if he allowed himself to become dehydrated.

Quincey knew how to live off the land. That had been part of his training as a Green Beret. The training had supplemented his interest in biology, making him self-sufficient in the wilderness. Although he had nothing but a pocketknife, he knew he could find food.

The palms had dropped coconuts, and he knew that their uncooked sprouts were quite nutritious. At a sandy spot on the riverbank, Quincey used a stick to uncover iguana eggs.

Without iodine tablets, Quincey couldn't drink the water from the river. Not only was his own survival at stake, but the survival of the children and the three volunteers. He had no intention of contracting a severe case of dysentery.

Instead, he searched until he found something that the natives called water vines. He used his pocketknife to make a tiny nick in the barklike stem. Quincey examined the first drop of liquid as it oozed out. It was clear. If it had been milky, it would likely have been poisonous.

He enlarged the hole and drank the pure water the vine offered. Two vines yielded sufficient moisture for the time being.

Next he cut a spear. Quincey smiled as he remembered doing the same thing in the same area less than a year ago. That time he'd had a larger knife for the job.

It took a long time to cut through the tough acacia sapling with a pocketknife, but when he was finished he had a seven-foot-long spear. Quincey decided to move upriver. He wanted to be quite a distance from the camp when he crossed back to that side of the river. He couldn't put a plan together until he had a clearer idea of the layout.

He waded through the Pomeroon and made his way slowly away from the camp. Although he burned to know what was happening, he didn't allow his sense of urgency to hurry his steps. He paused frequently to watch and listen.

It took all his will not to slap at the mosquitoes and stinging gnats that dogged him in the damp areas. His eyes constantly scanned the ground and trees for scorpions and snakes.

Each time he moved, the jungle noise in the immediate vicinity stopped. He thought of Able Team, which could move through the forest undetected. Their movements were so smooth and quiet that the birds paid them little if any attention.

It was late afternoon by the time he crossed the river and made his way back downstream to a place where he could see the clearing. The camp was quiet, too quiet. Only one person was in sight. Karen. The redheaded nurse was tied to the huge tree in the middle of the clearing. Quincey knew what their game was, and he knew he didn't have much time.

He turned to circle the camp, but came face-to-face with a mercenary who held a deadly PPSh-41 in his hands. Quincey hadn't used the Russian subgun before, but he recognized it. It was a product of the Second World War, no longer used by the Russians, but produced cheaply and sold to their allies. The thirty-five rounds of 7.62 mm bullets made very real holes in human flesh.

Quincey faced his captor, letting his spear drop to the ground between them, barely holding the end in his right hand. The grinning killer gestured with the PPSh-41 for Quincey to precede him into the compound.

CARL LYONS WALKED from the cockpit, his knees slightly bent against the air turbulence.

"Go talk to the army, Hal. They seem to want some sort of authorization before they'll okay us a helicopter."

The Fed raised an eyebrow, but he went forward.

Lyons dropped into his seat at the table and picked up the briefing. "Three men enter the restaurant just before it opens. The assistant cook picks up the day's supplies and arrives later. He hears gunshots as he arrives and signals a passing cop car. It was all luck and timing.

"The two squad cars on night duty had the place bottled up in less than a minute. The officers knew enough to let the gunmen know they were there. Probably saved a lot of lives. The three men figured hostages were more valuable than bodies.

"Place has only twenty-eight hundred people. The police requested state and federal help immediately. State police are backing up the town cops, but we get to clean up the mess."

"So how do we tango?"

Lyons shrugged. "Look first, make decisions later."

Brognola resumed his seat, before saying, "It's fixed. We land at Biggs Army Airfield in El Paso. An army helicopter takes us from there."

THE FOUR LANES OF HIGHWAY 10 SLASHED the Western town in half as if a giant combine had driven right up the middle.

The buildings lining the main street were one- or two-story wooden structures. Square boomtown fronts were commonplace. It was a slightly modernized version of the Wild West.

Police held the curious crowd a quarter of a mile back from the besieged restaurant. By the number of mounted men and women, it was obvious that horses were very much a part of daily life in this part of the country.

The restaurant was a one-story frame building that stretched a hundred and fifty feet back from the road. Its fresh white paint and classy sign spoke of prosperity.

Two state troopers cleared the highway a hundred yards behind the crowd of spectators. The Bell UH-1H Iroquois set down gently in the cleared area. The Able Team commandos were out and running before the engines were cut. They were almost up to the crowd before they heard the Lycoming turboshaft whine down.

They forced their way past a small group of people on horses and then past a gang of motorcyclists who stood astride their chromed machines, watching the hostage drama.

"Hey, man! Stop pushin' ahead," a biker growled.

Lyons looked the two-hundred-pound biker straight in the eyes and growled, "Feds. You want to help?"

The biker looked into the icy eyes and reevaluated the situation before asking, "Help? How?"

"I'll let you know," Lyons answered as his gaze transferred to the biker's Harley-Davidson Softail. The powerful machine was a tribute to its manufacturers.

A highway patrolman working crowd control moved to restrain Lyons, but was brushed aside.

"Where's Chief Daily?" the Stony Man warrior asked.

The state trooper looked at Lyons's jeans and plaid shirt and took in the stubble that covered the hard jaw. Then he remembered how easily he'd been swept aside and decided to let Daily sort it out.

"Over in the blue Ford," he told Lyons.

Three tough-looking men walked by him, followed by a petite oriental woman. The patrolman grabbed her arm.

"Where do you think you're going, little missy?"

She didn't even look at him, but twisted his arm as she broke out of the trooper's grasp. He felt his arm go numb as it dropped to his side.

"I'm with them," Lao said as she followed her Able Team comrades.

The patrolman rubbed his arm and looked at a fellow officer to his right.

"Shit," the patrolman said. "I'm glad those loonies inside the restaurant have to deal with those Feds and not me."

"They don't look that mean," his fellow officer said.

"Just stand back. They probably fart .45s."

Chief Daily might have been given his job in charge of Van Horn's four-man police force simply because he looked the part. He stood six foot three and added another six inches with his white Stetson and well-polished cowboy boots. He had wide shoulders and a narrow waist and hips. His smooth-shaven jaw was square and set as he emerged from his blue cruiser. One fist remained closed around the microphone for the cruiser's radio. The other held a Colt Python.

"I'm Carl Lyons," the Ironman told him.

"Shit. Your name don't matter none. Can you get those hostages out alive?"

"Can try."

"We tried telephoning the restaurant. They don't answer. You'll have to use a hailer to communicate."

Lyons ignored that avenue. "If they were to try blasting their way out, which way would be their best bet?"

"They got no bets. I got them sealed in tight."

Politician spoke hurriedly before Lyons could deliver blast, "You haven't missed anything. But if you were in their place, what would you try? What's their best bet?"

"Hanging tough. We ain't going to risk the hostages by going in. There's three of them and eleven prisoners. As long as they keep them real close, we haven't a prayer."

"And if they went loco, left their hostages and tried to blast their way out, which way would they have the most chance?" Politician insisted.

"I guess back through the rear and down the walkway to the next street. Got one car of state troopers there, but it's not really enough to seal it off. You figure on springing them?"

"Yeah. Here's what I want to do," Lyons began.

The big Texan listened impatiently, never taking his eyes off the restaurant.

"That's loco!" Chief Daily said for the tenth time as Lyons concluded his explanation.

"Have you got a better idea? You don't risk any Texan officers my way," Lyons said.

Daily laughed. "There is that to it. Go down the street to Lou's and tell him I said to loan you what you need. I'll ask the state boys to play your game."

"Not on the radio you won't. We're not a hundred percent sure they haven't an all-band receiver in there."

Daily flushed, but he pulled himself out of his cruiser and went to make arrangements.

As the Able Team warriors walked back toward the crowd, Gadgets said, "Why the risk? I could get in there after dark."

"We need one alive. Those three are only the henchmen. Somebody else is planning the executions. Besides they don't answer the telephone," Lyons growled.

"Huh?"

"When hostages-takers don't talk, they're waiting for something."

By then they were back among the motorcycle riders.

"We want to borrow three bikes and jackets," Lyons told the leader.

"What are you going to do?"

"Spring the guys inside."

"Horseshit. I heard you tell the cop you're a Fed."

"We're going to spring them anyway. We'll be wearing your jackets. Want the publicity?"

"This I got to see!" the burly leader exclaimed, stripping off his jacket.

Lyons turned to Lao Ti as he put on the jacket. "I want you on a roof on the next street. Pretend to keep the cops pinned. Stay on your communicator."

Lao shrugged and marched back to the helicopter for her H&K caseless.

Five minutes later, still surrounded by the crowd, Lyons, Blancanales and Schwarz wore jackets identifying them as members of the Destroyers, a motorcycle club in Texas. Lyons and Blancanales eased their cycles back to the horsemen. Gadgets drove on to the sporting goods store.

"Want to help?" Lyons asked the riders.

"What do you have in mind?"

"In five minutes we're going to come through here doing eighty. We don't want to kill anyone."

"Roundup time," one of them laughed. "Who are you guys anyway?"

Blancanales made a show of squinting at Lyons's jacket. "The Destroyers."

The horsemen laughed again but began using their cow ponies to push the crowd to either side.

Lyons and Politician made their way to a pay phone in a service station lot. They stood by the phone and waited. Five minutes later they heard the sound of breaking glass.

Politician immediately dialed the number of the restaurant where the hostages were being held. The telephone rang and rang before it was finally answered.

"Yes? Who is this?"

"You got the note?"

"I answered the telephone, didn't I? The note on the arrow said you could help. Who are you?"

"Your way out," Politician told him. "Someone's paying a lot of money for you. We're going to come right up to the front door. Let us in. Don't shoot."

"We don't need your tricks."

"Shit, man. You hang up and you lose us ten big ones, and you lose your lives. Don't be a cow's ass."

Politician finally placed the trace of an accent. He racked his brains for a few words of Arabic.

"The guy who hired us gave us a message for you." Politician deliberately paused, then stumbled over the words. "Allah at-bar."

"Was that *Allah Akbar*?"

"Yeah. That sounds like it," Blancanales confirmed.

"I can see why he didn't entrust you with a more complex message. What do you plan to do?" The voice was calm.

"I got someone on a roof to hold back the pigs. We're coming in the front and out the back before these hicks know what hit them. It's all timing. You gotta be ready to jump. But the whole thing's off when the Feds get here."

"How many of you?"

"Three."

"Come ahead. If this is a trick, many die."

"Shit, man. If this is a trick, I die. The man said he'd get us out of here once we're clear of town."

"Come ahead."

The cool hostage-taker hung up the telephone.

Gadgets pulled up on his borrowed Harley. "Hey, this thing will hit ninety in under seven seconds," he crowed.

"Then you win the honor of leading the way," Lyons said in a dry voice.

"That's the last time I brag about anything," Gadgets complained. But he drew his MAC-10 and gunned the engine.

Politician produced a mini-Uzi and clamped it between his thigh and the gas tank. Ironman held his Colt Python in his right hand, using the friction of his wrist to turn the accelerator.

The three big bikes leaped ahead and roared down the middle of the highway. The crowd magically parted in front of them. The powerful machines swept through in single file doing well over fifty miles an hour. When they burst into the cleared area, they expended a number of shells over the spectators' heads. The crowd stampeded for cover, and the policemen hit the dirt.

They barely had time to tuck their weapons between leg and gas tank before they were up to the front door of the building. Already the police were firing after them, and bullets raised dust at the edge of the road.

At the last possible moment the front door to the restaurant was yanked open and the three drove through. Chairs and tables were overturned as the men braked the big bikes.

Three men in jeans and cowboy shirts covered them with 9 mm Stechkin automatics. The hostages were lined up against the broken window in the front of the restaurant. Two men lay dead on the floor.

"Get the back door open," Lyons shouted. "We've got three seconds until the cops figure out what's happening."

"Tell us what—" a hostage-taker began.

Lyons interrupted. "This bike moves in two more seconds whether you're on it or not. Get that fucking door open."

When the terrorists stayed rooted to the spot, Lyons snapped the clutch and gunned the engine. The heavy Harley spat pieces of rug as it charged down the narrow hall toward the door to the rear parking lot. At the last moment Lyons braked the rear wheel and smashed the door off its hinges.

He looked back and shouted, "Last chance."

Two of the terrorists swung on behind Gadgets and Politician. The leader sprinted for Lyons's Harley. The terrorist on Blancanales's cycle lined up on the waitresses huddled in the corner.

"Don't be a fool!" Politician snapped and started accelerating.

The killer had to forget shooting in order to hold on. The leader was almost boosted onto the Harley by Pol's front wheel. The three cycles roared into the parking area, spinning dirt behind them.

Lyons headed straight toward the walkway leading to the next street. The terrorists suddenly doubted the ability of the big machines to go through the narrow space between the buildings. At forty miles an hour, Ironman led the way, his handlebars only four inches from each wall. One false move and the machine would hit the side.

They burst out of the alley like wasps streaming from the entrance to their hive. The two officers covering the street already had their revolvers out, but a sudden burst of autofire from a roof sent them diving for cover.

"Aiiiyeee!" a terrorist shouted. "Free!"

Lyons turned northwest. A moving van blocked most of the street, but there was ample room for the motorcycles to maneuver around it. Ironman was wondering how the hell he was going to get the alert terrorist off his back. The problem resolved itself.

The terrorist leaned forward and shouted in his ear, "I didn't believe you until I saw the van. Stop."

Puzzled, Lyons pulled up. The other cycles stopped behind him. The three terrorists jumped off the seats and ran toward the van.

The back door flew up, and two submachine guns opened fire on Able Team.

3

Pat Quincey's captor motioned for him to go ahead into the camp.

The minister bent as if to put down his spear. When his hand was a few inches from the ground, he whipped up the tip of the spear and lunged, bringing the spear smashing into the Russian-made subgun. The weapon was jolted against the goon's chest, and he was driven back.

Quincey slid his left hand up the shaft and swung the tip of the spear against the gunman's wrists, knocking the weapon farther to one side. He followed the swing of the spear by charging the goon, knocking him off his feet. Quincey lashed out with his boot, finally managing to knock the weapon out of the hands of the man in black.

Heavy footfalls thumping through the rain forest told Quincey that their encounter had been heard. He had no time to finish the kill or to pick up the weapon. He took off, spear still in his hands.

When he found his way blocked by a fallen tree, Quincey used the spear to vault over it. He left the spear, sprinted to the river and dived in. The swift river currents swept him around a bend, taking him out of sight of his pursuers.

He rested on the far bank before returning to the river. Pursuit was close; he could tell from the voices that they had reached the bank upriver.

Quincey swam back across the Pomeroon. It swept him ahead of his pursuers. He climbed out through weeds where his tracks were less noticeable. The killers had spotted his prints on the far bank. Quincey could hear them wading into the river.

Moving cautiously, Quincey circled back toward the camp a second time. This time he spotted a sentry before the man spotted him. Quincey smiled grimly. It was unlikely that he'd drawn enough thugs from the camp to slip in unnoticed. The well-trained sentries hadn't left their posts.

The ex-Green Beret quietly slipped away. The river bowed around the camp, isolating it on three sides. Quincey waded into the river on the opposite side of the camp and swam as far as he could underwater before stroking quietly to the far bank. By the time he eased himself out of the water, he was opposite the camp in the center of the bow.

He decided to move into the forest away from the camp until the pursuit died down. He moved slowly, listening, watching for poisonous snakes. He also kept alert for parrots or packs of monkeys. If he disturbed them, they'd tell the entire district where he was.

Quincey weighed his options once more. It would take him several days to reach Georgetown. He couldn't hope for any help from the authorities. Did he dare to stay away for several days? If only Able Team were here now.

How long would it take Karen to succumb to exposure? How long would it be before anyone realized their return was overdue and come looking?

Quincey decided to stay around. He'd watch for a break. He couldn't just abandon Karen and the children.

Why did thinking of Karen make him feel like rushing the camp and cracking skulls? If no one noticed that their group was missing, Quincey knew he would have made the wrong decision.

He found an area of thinner vegetation, full of new growth. There were enough dry leaves and twigs on the ground to warn him of human approach. He set about to make another spear.

LAO TI LAY on the flat graveled roof of a two-story building. Below her was a small vegetable garden. The potatoes had just been harvested and the pitchfork left at one corner of the garden. Farther along the street was the highway patrol car and two lanky Texans, nervously watching the walkway from the parking lot behind the restaurant.

Twice the officers pulled their revolvers, then put them back. Lao wondered if it had been a mistake to let them in on the plan to separate the killers from their hostages. The roar of the motorcycles echoing between the buildings interrupted her thoughts.

She peppered the street with 4.7 mm rounds, bringing them close enough to the police officers' feet to make their dive for cover look very realistic. Then she ran toward the outside stairs to make her way to the helicopter.

That's when she heard the cycles slow down. She paused and looked, but another building obstructed her view. When three subguns suddenly opened up, Lao knew there was trouble. She took the steps two at a time.

LYONS, BLANCANALES AND SCHWARZ had each clamped his weapon between his leg and the motorcycle's gas tank before they'd driven out of the restaurant. When the killers leaped from the backs of the motorcycles, the members of Able Team were already reaching for their weapons. When the back door of the van was flung open, they rolled clear of the motorcycles, letting them drop.

The big motorcycles were little protection from a hail of 7.62 mm heart-stoppers, but they were all Able Team had. They took cover behind the bikes and raised their weapons to send the killers their compliments.

The Libyan killmasters had thrown open the rear door of the van five seconds too soon. Their own men were in the way and had to dive clear. This prevented them from coordinating their attack with the subgunners in the van.

The two who fired on Able Team stood in the rear of the van, confident of a sudden kill. More men huddled in the darkness near the front of the truck box, content to stay clear. Three men, armed only with Stechin automatics, stood behind the subgunners, waiting to help their fellow killers into the truck.

The Russian army stopped using the PPSh-41s because of their tendency to stargaze. Able Team went down as their enemy's death-spitting SMG muzzles went up. The gunmen had set the two weapons on automatic, avoiding the error of using the full cyclic rate. Still, by the time they brought their line of fire down to Able Team's level, the three terror fighters had joined in the debate.

Lyons's Python spoke first, two deep-throated booms speaking out above the stuttering of the subguns. His shots were snapped off quickly because he was more concerned with interrupting the killers' concentration than with slower, more accurate shooting. The .45s perforated the roof of the van. The Libyans jerked back, losing the fight to line up their weapons.

The three men who had been sprung by Able Team dived and rolled, frantic to get out of the way of the hellfire coming from their comrades. It wasn't until they had rolled twelve to fifteen feet from the fire zone that they thought of joining the battle.

Gadgets sliced a line of fire across the van with his MAC-10. The Libyans were already jerking back from Lyons's fire. The three backup men threw themselves flat. Gadgets's .45s removed a PPSh-41 from one killer's hands, but they failed to chew flesh.

Able Team was in a bad way. They didn't have time for careful shooting and they didn't have the ammunition to keep up the barrage. The three had fired a great deal of their ammunition to make a good impression when they'd rode up to the restaurant. There hadn't been any time to reload their weapons.

Politician decided he had to take more time with his mini-Uzi. The other two had bought him precious seconds by firing quickly. It was up to him to make the kills. He sighted in on the killer who still held his subgun and squeezed the trigger.

Return fire from a Stechkin automatic, roaring at the full cyclic rate of 750 rounds per minute, found the gas tank on Pol's bike and chewed it to bits. Politician instinctively recoiled and rolled away. The next bullets, from another handgun, ignited the spilled gas.

The Libyan kill-squad member who still held his subgun saw Politician lining up on him and leaped away from the door. The three hostage-takers dashed for the van, firing their Stechkins as they ran. The three backup men crawled forward to offer the runners a hand up.

Gadgets's machine pistol clicked back on an empty clip just as the van started to pull away.

LAO TI JUMPED down the last remaining steps and landed in the freshly dug earth. She tucked and rolled, hugging the H&K caseless across her chest. The roll brought her to her feet, and she quickly rounded the building that had blocked her view in time to see Politician roll away from a motorcycle just before the spilled gasoline turned to flame. She was also aware that Gadgets's weapon was empty.

One killer still had bullets in his automatic. He too was aware that Gadgets and Politician were in no position to fire back at him. He stopped, took a two-handed firing stance and lined up on Lyons.

The time he took proved fatal. Lao's caseless growled, and two figure-eight 4.7 mm death-stings straightened him up.

Two blasts from Lyons's Colt removed the back of the killer's head and dumped him over backward.

The van peeled rubber, and none of Able Team's weapons had any lead left to dissuade it.

The two officers from the street behind the restaurant were the first to reach the scene. Brognola was right behind them with his Police Special in his fist. The Able Team warriors were concentrating on reloading their weapons.

"What happened?" Brognola demanded.

"They had a backup crew and escape vehicle. We took them right to it," Lyons said. He turned to a patrolman. "Get us to the chopper, fast."

As the policeman sprinted for his vehicle, Lyons asked Brognola, "Can you stay long enough to straighten out this mess with the owners?" Ironman gestured toward the bullet-riddled motorcycles.

Brognola nodded as he returned his revolver to its belt holster.

"Get them," he told Able Team.

Despite the siren, it took at least six minutes to get through the crowd to the chopper. It was another six before the engine was warmed up enough for them to take to the air. The patrol cars were slowly making their way through the crowds. By the time they were free, they'd lost track of the moving van.

While the state police radioed to have all units watch for the van, the army helicopter swept the main highways.

"We have to return for fuel," the pilot reported.

"Do it, but radio ahead to have two more choppers warmed up and ready. We have to find that van." Lyons's voice was grim. "When you're refueled, go back for Brognola. He's the one who takes care of the authorizations."

"I haven't the authority to make those arrangements, sir."

"Get me through to your flight command. I have," Lyons growled.

It took ten minutes, but finally he reached the camp commander. "Either have those choppers waiting or have a message for me from the White House telling me to no longer pursue the matter," Lyons demanded.

The commander spluttered something, but Lyons merely handed the microphone back to the pilot.

"That's a major general on the radio, sir."

"Tell him to get off. You'll need the radio for identifying yourself when we come over the base."

The pilot glared at Lyons, but diplomatically did as he was told.

Almost one hour after taking off from Van Horn and the landing to refuel, Able Team were in the air again. Lyons and Lao rode one chopper, Blancanales and Gadgets in another.

Twenty minutes later a highway patrol spotted the van coming out of the Hueco Mountains, approaching El Paso International Airport. Pol and Gadgets were ten minutes away. Lyons and Lao would take nearly a half hour to reach the airport. Brognola had been picked up and was headed back to Biggs Army Airfield, adjacent to the El Paso airport.

Working through the radio operator at Biggs, Brognola coordinated a massive police effort to stop the killers. There were no confrontations. The experienced Fed started at the top and cajoled, never openly using his connection to the White House. He didn't have to.

Airport security, state troopers and El Paso police threw a net around the airport and moved in. No one boarded a plane without a ticket. Everyone buying a ticket was carefully scrutinized. If there was any doubt, they were held for identification.

The helicopter carrying Gadgets and Politician was allowed to land near the main terminal. Just as they were touching down, airport security reported that the van had been found. It had been driven into some trees a half mile from the passenger terminal.

A security officer was waiting for the Iroquois to land. If Politician's and Gadgets's unshaven, unkempt condition aroused the security officer's suspicion, he didn't show it. He gave them security badges that they pinned on their shirts and led them to the lounge where airport security was holding people for them to check.

The two Stony Man warriors quickly decided that none of the people being held had been involved in the Van Horn shoot-out. They toured the terminal and grounds, but saw no sign of their quarry. Occasionally they'd be asked to check someone else, but without result.

Brognola arrived, then Lyons and Lao. The five expanded their search area. Police still stopped all cars leaving their dragnet, but without results.

Three hours later Brognola called off the search. The airport's schedule was behind time because of the police lines. The area had been searched, and Brognola was reasonably certain the killers hadn't surfaced within the tightening perimeter.

Lyons, using his security badge as a passport, strode into the control tower and demanded a list of all planes that had taken off in the last three hours. He scanned it, then stabbed a powerful finger down on six departures one after another, demanding details. Three were private planes too small to carry a group the size of the terrorists. Two had left from the freight terminal, and one was a charter flight to Cuba.

"Stop that Cuban flight," Lyons demanded.

"Can't. It's already in international air space. Besides, everyone was aboard before the alert."

Lyons swore.

"I want details on the freighters."

"Courtney Air Freight. One-man operation. Specializes in rush charters for industry. Picks up computer parts and that sort of thing."

"Big enough to take our killers?"

"Well, yeah. It's a Volpar Turbo 18. It could take six people, but it's outfitted for two passengers and cargo. Besides, most of the boys here know Courtney. He wouldn't get involved in anything like that."

"Where's he headed?"

The chief controller looked at his notes. "Mexico. He'll be on the ground by now. Want me to try to reach him?"

Lyons didn't answer. His finger stabbed the last questioned departure hard enough to crumple the paper.

"And this one?"

"Oh, that. Landed early this morning to distribute free samples of fresh shrimp to the restaurants. It was all set to take off before the alert came through. Took off from the freight terminal."

"Big enough to take fifteen or twenty men?"

"Hell, it was a 747-SP. Could have taken more than a hundred men. First SP I saw converted for freight. Dozen salesmen and crew. As I said, they were all on board when the call came through."

"Then why didn't it leave right away?"

"Huh?"

"Time puts takeoff a half hour after the alert."

"Oh, yeah. Pilot had some sort of computer trouble. Delayed takeoff until he could double-check the programming."

"Have that plane forced to land before it leaves the country."

The chief controller went over to one of the radar screens and spoke to the operator. His expression told Lyons what he'd half expected.

"Too late. The plane's already over South America. Those birds go fast and they go far. It'll set down in Georgetown in half an hour."

Lyons delivered an icy stare and stalked out of the tower.

"They could have disappeared on one of three flights," Lyons reported to Brognola. "Though only part of the group could have gone on Courtney Air Freight. Don't know how so many men could get through the net."

"You saved the hostages," Brognola reminded Ironman.

"They got their target. How many more get killed before we stop them?"

Brognola couldn't answer. He silently led the way back to the waiting army helicopters.

FROM WHERE SHE WAS TIED to the tree in the center of the compound, Karen Yates was aware of almost everything that happened in camp. The late afternoon chase reached her ears. She didn't see Quincey, but she was sure she knew what had happened. Maybe he was correct to stay free. But she needed his help to reach the radio.

Mugarieff ordered Lisa Frane to spoon-feed Karen a small supper. Frane completed the task in a grim, business-like way.

"Still think we need to hold out?" Frane asked.

"What else would you suggest?"

"Maybe if we just cooperated."

"We'll cooperate until we can get a message out."

"Fat chance," Frane said, ending the conversation.

Two Libyan soldiers untied Karen, led her to and from the latrine, and retied her to the tree. The knots didn't cut off her circulation, but they didn't leave her any hope of escape, either.

At sunset George returned. He had left with six Muslim fanatics. He returned with eighteen. When Karen saw his stiff-legged walk, she knew George was in a foul temper. Mugarieff reported to him immediately. George glared her way, but didn't approach her right away.

After a five-minute conversation with Mugarieff, Yates strode off to the Quonset hut and dragged Frane out. He hustled her over to the barracks building and stayed there for half an hour. Only after he had walked Frane back to the chldren did George come over to stand in front of Karen. He scowled at her before he spoke.

"You had to be smart and Mugarieff had to be chicken-hearted. Well, your boyfriend seems to be snapping at the bait, so I'll let his decision stand. I'm going to Washington to complete some unfinished business."

He turned and strutted off, shouting orders.

Karen tugged at her bonds. Did George's trip have anything to do with Able Team? Would Pat walk into the trap when she started to sag? Desperate, she tugged at her bonds until her chafed wrists bled. The ropes didn't loosen.

4

The 747 with the blue belly and red stripes taxied slowly toward the freight section of the field. Bold blue letters proclaimed that the plane belonged to Guyana Seafood Specialties. A large pink shrimp adorned the forty-foot-high tail of the aircraft.

A ten-foot-high cargo door opened behind the starboard wing. A refrigerated truck backed up to the cargo door and waited. Attendants from a plane service company wheeled a set of steps up to a passenger door just behind and below the cockpit. The steps met the sill of the door exactly.

Within minutes, yellow lights blinking, a customs vehicle sped up to the plane. A customs officer and a food inspector hurried up the steps. The passenger door didn't open until they were at the top of the portable steps.

The tall man with the build of a line-destroying quarterback stood in the doorway. He wore a dark suit, white shirt and a brilliant jade tie. His shoes gleamed in the airport lights.

"Good evening, gentlemen. Thank you for arriving so promptly," he told the inspectors. His voice was smooth, relaxed.

"What sort of foodstuffs are you carrying?"

"Fresh shrimp."

The food inspector automatically sniffed the air, although they were standing in the first-class cabin. There were about twenty men sitting in the section, craning their necks and watching the transaction. Each was dressed in a conservative suit and all wore identically striped ties.

"This plane carries both passengers and cargo? I haven't seen a 747-SP converted for cargo before," the customs man said.

He was rewarded with another dazzling smile. "We believe this is the first. Actually, only the three forward first-class decks have been kept for passengers. The rest of the space is for cargo. I have my entire sales force here. We'll distribute the free samples to restaurants in and around Washington as they open. In about a week we'll come back and take orders. We expect to fly in a planeload a day soon. You just can't get the same flavor from frozen shrimp."

It was after midnight. Neither inspector wanted to drag out the process.

"Fine. How long do you intend to stay?" the customs inspector asked.

"We should be taking off again between one and three this afternoon. That depends on how soon your better restaurants open."

"The plane will stay here during that time?"

"Naturally. It will be cleaned, provisioned and refueled for the return flight. The crew have hotel rooms waiting."

The two inspectors exchanged glances. With a multimillion dollar plane as surety, their job would be considerably easier.

"Why don't you look at the cargo while I talk to the salesmen and the crew?" the customs inspector said to his companion.

The food inspector nodded and gestured for the man to lead the way to the cargo holds.

About two hundred wooden crates of shrimp and cracked ice were neatly stowed just behind the passenger section. The crates occupied only a small area of the large hold.

"That's all the cargo you're carrying?"

"Yes. That's all we feel we can distribute initially. To be a success our product must remain fresh. Soon, we hope to make daily deliveries with ten times the amount of shrimp for the Washington area, and eventually we hope to expand to other cities. Truly fresh shrimp every day, not frozen."

The inspector was growing tired of the sales pitch. He opened a crate and picked up a shrimp to examine it. It was firm. Only hours out of the water. Shrimp boats stayed out five days at a time, beheading shrimp and packing them in ice as they were caught. Anything that had only been out of the water for six days was considered fresh. These were more than fresh.

"Import permit," he requested.

It was produced immediately.

"I suppose you'll want lab tests. We have an empty crate. Why don't you scoop your samples into that?"

"Don't need samples. Your papers and inspections are all in order."

"Oh." The man sounded disappointed. "I had them load two more cases than we need. I'll probably have to get rid of them. How do I do that?"

"You'll throw two cases away?"

The man shrugged. "We don't freeze and we don't deliver more than twenty-four hours after the shrimp boats come in. Even the boats aren't allowed to stay out more than three days. I don't suppose you could get rid of them for me. It seems such a shame to waste all that food."

The inspector poked his hand into a box. It encountered nothing but shrimp, ice and plastic liner. "Sounds like a bribe."

"It isn't. It's a request for a favor. Why don't I carry it down and ask everyone on duty to take some? You should be able to find bags or something to put them in. I don't want to do anything that isn't aboveboard."

"Ah, hell, let's see what Al says."

They returned to the passenger section. The customs man was just coming down the spiral stairs from the upper lounges and the cockpit.

"All the sales force are Guyanese. The crew's American. Passports are all in order." He looked at the man in charge. "Are you Guyanese as well?"

"Hell, no. I'm American. Just working down there as sales manager." He reached into his jacket pocket and produced a worn passport. "Name's George, George Yates."

The customs man took a quick look at the passport.

"Mr. Yates brought two extra cases of fresh shrimp. He thought we'd want lab tests," the food inspector said.

The customs and immigration man gave Yates a suspicious look. "So?"

"So he's offered to carry the cases around and offer some to everyone on duty."

"I guess we can do that for him," the customs man conceded.

"First two down the chute," Yates promised.

By the time the inspectors reached the ground again, a chute had been lowered to the waiting refrigerated truck. The first crates down the chute were turned over to the two inspectors, who looked forward to a meal of expensive shrimp. As they drove away, case after case swished down the chute into the truck.

One salesman climbed in beside the truck driver. The rest walked through the freight building to where a rental agent was waiting with ten passenger cars. He accepted an American Express voucher and watched the men drive off.

"Strange," he muttered to himself. "Not one of them was over thirty-five."

Once clear of the airport, the cars and truck all headed south or west. They traveled at different speeds and selected a variety of routes. No visible convoy moved southwest from Washington, but all the vehicles converged again in an industrial park on the northern fringe of Charlottesville, Virginia.

The truck backed up to the shipping door of a small unit in an industrial plaza. The driver climbed down and unlocked both the regular door and the shipping door.

George Yates and the others followed him into the building. It was empty except for three used vans.

"Hope it's okay. About the only thing for rent in the city," the driver said. "I bought the vans and stole the plates only a few hours ago. They won't be missed yet. The garbage bags are by the door."

"It'll do," George told him. He turned to the men with him. "Go," he told them.

The cases were dragged from the truck and unpacked. A plastic bag of weapons or ammunition was fished from the bottom of each crate. The shrimp and ice were then poured into plastic garbage bags and set back into the truck.

When they were through, each man held a PPSh-41, two spare clips and a Stechin. The extra weapons and ammunition were put into garbage bags and stored in the empty crates in one corner of the open area. Anyone taking a casual look would see only a pile of smelly, discarded crates.

George Yates then dispatched a van with four Libyan killers to follow the truck.

"Get rid of the garbage bags in a suburb expecting garbage pickup this morning," Yates instructed. "Then return the truck to the rental agency and join us at the church. Remember to hang back until we're engaged. Got it?"

The truck driver nodded and translated for the few Libyans in the group who couldn't follow Yates's instructions.

When the truck pulled away from the large door, the terrorists drove the vans out and parked the rented cars inside.

They then stripped off their business clothes and left them in the small office area. They wore light gray battle fatigues. On their heads they wore headbands that could be unrolled into full face masks. George Yates, dressed like his men, led the way to the other vans.

Two of the killers carried a field mortar.

HAL BROGNOLA POUNDED on Lyons's door at Stony Man farm. It was 0300 hours.

"Yeah. Come in," Lyons's deep, sleepy voice muttered.

"Like hell," Hal Brognola shouted through the closed door. "I'm not about to get my head shot off."

The door opened quietly, and Ironman stood there, naked except for the Colt Python that filled his fist.

"What's up, Hal?" Lyons voice held no trace of the faked sleepiness that had invited the Fed inside.

"I'm not sure. It may be the men we're looking for. Briefing in five minutes," Hal said in a loud voice.

He spoke loudly for the benefit of the rest of the team. He knew the commotion of getting Ironman up would have Blancanales, Schwarz and Lao on full alert. They were already standing in the doorways of their rooms. Each had a weapon in one hand.

Brognola pulled his dressing gown tighter as he stomped away. He was wondering why he never sent a security type to enjoy the hair-raising experience of waking Able Team.

Five minutes later Able Team and Brognola met in the war room. The night cook put an insulated jug of coffee on the table and retreated to the kitchen.

Lyons poured himself a mug of coffee. He slurped down a mouthful, taking plenty of air through the liquid to get it down while it was still hot.

"Shoot," he told Brognola.

The head Fed was neatly dressed but unshaven. He brought his coffee mug to his lips, decided it was much too hot, and set it down again.

"Someone lobbed mortars into Pat Quincey's home in Charlottesville."

"Good thing he's in Guyana with those kids," Politician said.

"What about the church?" Ironman asked.

Brognola took a moment to try to follow Lyons's jump in thinking. "It's okay as far as I know. Why?"

"What's the point unless they hit the church?"

Brognola digested that for a few seconds before asking, "Do you think they're delivering a message?"

"Why use a mortar when a can of gasoline will do the same thing?"

"I don't get it," Gadgets said. "If they did use a mortar for a calling card, why take out the church?"

"Just checking," Lyons said. "If the church is okay, the church is the trap."

"For us?" Lao asked. "Who associates us with Quincey?"

"Rising Sons. Karen Yates's husband."

Politician didn't like the way the conversation was going. "You're accusing Karen of giving us away."

"Maybe she was careless. No one has been here, yet."

"Are you saying someone may raid Stony Man?" Brognola demanded.

"They'd be here by now. I'm saying Karen let something slip about Quincey. She's with him. She isn't going around blabbing."

"Let's look. Then theorize," Gadgets said.

Able Team started to stand up, but Brognola barked, "Just a damn second. This sounds a little farfetched. But if Carl's right, you're walking into a trap."

"Yeah," Lyons answered.

Brognola sighed. "I'll order a helicopter."

"Don't bother," Blancanales answered. "This time of night it's just as fast to take the van. It's less conspicuous."

Brognola thought about that. By the time he decided Politician was right, Able Team had gone for their weapons.

Politician guided Able Team's van through the sixty-mile journey from Stony Man to Charlottesville. Twice they had to exchange radio messages with the state police to get cruisers off their tail.

When he reached Charlottesville, Politician slowed the van down to the speed limit. He wanted to approach the church as discreetly as possible.

"How do we handle this?" Gadgets asked.

Lyons looked at the quiet grounds around the darkened church. The church hall had been repaired since Able Team had last prevented the Guyana-based religious cult from assassinating the Reverend Patrick Quincey. The church hall had taken three HE missiles when the cult's backup crew had tried to kill Quincey.

"We'll go right through the middle," Lyons decided. "Park the van. We walk. We work toward the van, not away."

Politician drove past the church without slowing. He found a service station that had closed for the night and left the van there. They packed their long weapons into a sports bag that Lyons carried. Then the four warriors, in gray combat fatigues, casually walked through side streets until they reached the far side of the church.

They met only two pedestrians who stared at the strange outfits and hastened their steps. The few cars that passed neither slowed down nor increased their speed.

Once on the other side of the church, they crossed the road and entered the grounds. When they were in the shadows, Lyons opened the sports bag and distributed the weapons.

Gadgets attached a clip to his right thigh. It held his favorite weapon, the MAC-10 .45 caliber subgun. His silenced Beretta already rode under his fatigues.

Lao accepted the H&K caseless, which she'd kept since their trip to England. The female commando had chosen to experiment with a smaller personal weapon. She carried a new Colt Government Model .380 in a belt holster under her fatigues. She could reach it quickly through the irregularly spaced front buttons of her camous.

Politician accepted his trusted M-16 with attached M-203 grenade launcher. He wore a mini-Uzi in a swivel holster under his right arm. The holster allowed the weapon to be swung up with the right hand and fired almost instantly.

Lyons kept the Colt Python under his left arm. He pulled his Konzak battle shotgun from the sports bag and tossed the bag to one side. He'd fitted the Konzak with a twenty-round drum of his usual mix of Number Two and Double O shot.

Able Team spread out. Lyons moved up the middle toward the flat-roofed hall and office building. Schwarz and Blancanales took wing positions, ten feet back and fifteen feet to each side. Lao Ti, thirty feet back from Lyons, spent most of her time watching their back trail.

When trouble came, it arrived quietly.

As Lao checked to the right, a shadow moved from the tree to her left. Whether the attacker made some slight noise in the dew-covered grass or her instincts warned her of the attack, Lao whirled, raising the arm holding the H&K caseless.

The plastic casing of the gun intercepted a hand that came at her with such force that it knocked the weapon from her grip. The attacker followed the punch with a roundhouse kick aimed at the crotch.

Lao spun with the blow that knocked the rifle out of her hand. Her right fist crashed into the ninja's calf, speeding his kick so it brushed past her harmlessly. Off-balance, the silent attacker took a giant step to move himself out of Lao's reach. It was the wrong move.

Lao lunged, using a front snap kick that reached farther than her arm could. Her combat boot broke two ribs. The ninja staggered then fell on his face.

Two more camou-clad figures leaped from the trees, landing on Politician and Gadgets.

Blancanales reacted quickly, bringing up his M-16 and pressing it against the force of the attack. The barrel caught the ninja on the bridge of the nose, smashing him back before his deadly blow could connect.

Gadgets was thrown off his feet, but he managed to fend off a lethal blow with his left hand while his right swung the MAC-10 toward the attacker. A trio of .45s showed the Libyan assassination expert the error of his ways by blasting pieces from his chest.

Lyons heard the fighting break out behind him. Instinctively he raised the Konzak and put two blasts into the elm just ahead of him. Leaves, twigs and two pieces of rotten fruit in night-camou fatigues dropped from the tree.

The sound of Able Team's return fire told the ninja that their stealthy attack wasn't working as they had hoped. PPSh-41s began to pepper the night with 7.62 mm Soviet-made propaganda.

Lao made a long dive for her dropped weapon. The Libyan ninja with the broken ribs scrambled on all fours to intercept her. The only thing he intercepted was a salvo of bullets directed at Lao.

Lao managed to grab her H&K but had to keep rolling away from streams of autofire that came at her from two directions.

Blancanales followed through with a kick that smashed his opponent's pelvic bone. Even as he delivered a finishing stomp to the solar plexus, the white-haired warrior was reaching for a wire-wound grenade and loading the M-203.

Gadgets stayed on the ground, aiming and firing short bursts at any muzzle-flashes he could see. His Ingram was soon empty. He was reaching for another clip when he spotted the van coming across the grass. He shouted a warning as he calmly continued changing clips.

Ironman continued toward the defoliated tree. He snapped a blast of Double O and Number Two pellets at each muzzle-flash. When he reached the tree, he stood with his back to it and continued to fire until the drum was empty. He was yanking the drum free, preparing to slam home a fresh one, when Gadgets called his warning.

Politician swung around toward the speeding van. Already, darkly dressed reinforcements were jumping out of the moving vehicle. A tight figure eight of .223 tumblers ruined the windshield and did little for the driver's health.

The Able Team warrior's right hand slid forward to the trigger of the grenade launcher. The wire-wound flew straight through the shattered windshield and helped the last three assassins out of the van. A short flash lit the interior, and three bodies tumbled from the side door and lay where they fell. The van bucked twice and stopped.

Lao rolled and came to a sitting position with her caseless in her hands. She stitched three Libyans who had been about to riddle Politician. They flopped back without firing. Two of them wouldn't get up again.

Ironman's clip clicked home, and the Konzak started once more to persuade the terror killers to give up.

"They're pulling back," Lao shouted.

Able Team advanced cautiously, meeting only light resistance from the enemy. At the end of the church grounds, two gunners fired in their direction. Able Team had an open stretch ahead of them and were pinned. Beyond the gunners, two engines roared to life.

Politician used the launcher to place a grenade behind one position. The scream and gurgle told Able Team they had melted one point of resistance. They spread out and moved in on the last gunner.

The firing broke off suddenly, and they charged as he was ramming home a fresh clip. There was a single shot. The last gunman lay beside his dead comrades. He had fired once into his own mouth.

The rest of the pseudo-ninjas took off in their vans.

Sirens sounded from all sides of the churchyard.

5

"Shit!" exclaimed the first policeman on the scene. "It's that bulletproof Fed again."

"At least the buildings haven't been blown up," his partner said. The last time Able Team had fought a battle on those grounds, the church hall had been hit with antitank missiles. The police officer's voice didn't reflect much consolation in the unscathed condition of the buildings.

"Radio the airport," Lyons ordered them. "Find out if they have a charter from Cuba, a plane from Courtney Air Freight or a 747-SP there right now."

The two policemen exchanged glances.

"You really want us to try to get all that through our dispatcher?" the older cop asked.

Other cruisers came up over the grounds, bathing Able Team in the glare of their high beams.

"Throw down those guns," a policeman ordered from behind the glare of his headlights.

"Save your breath, O'Hanna," the young cop who'd encountered Able Team before shouted. "They won't do it."

"You know them?" the voice rose half an octave.

"No one knows these guys, but the Feds let them run loose."

While the police were trying to decide what to do, Gadgets had his communicator out. It took a while to find the frequency for the control tower at the Charlottesville-Albemarle Airport. It took even longer to get the tower to cooperate. But he finally received the information he wanted.

"None of the planes you want are at Charlottesville," Gadgets reported.

Three cruisers were sitting on the church grounds with their lights on. The police were still discussing Able Team as if they weren't there. The two officers who had seen the grounds after the last battle took great delight in giving their co-workers all the gory details once again.

A few neighbors began to collect, many in dressing gowns. Suddenly a woman began to scream.

"What's that?" a policeman said.

"She saw a body," Lao Ti, who had just circled the church, told him.

"A body? There's a corpse here?"

"Eight or ten," she answered.

"Can you get through to Stony Man?" Lyons asked Gadgets.

"Yeah, no problem."

The police were trying to move people off the grounds in order to search the bodies.

"Have them check all the airports in the area for those damn planes. Put Grimaldi on alert. Get a chopper here to pick us up fast. Have them send someone to take the van back." Lyons snapped off the string of orders as if they were routine.

Gadgets nodded and got to work.

"What happened here?" a policeman demanded.

"They were littering," Lyons quipped. He refused to answer another question.

Brognola arrived shortly after with the Hughes Model 500-D helicopter. The twenty-six-foot rotors were small enough to let the bubble-shaped craft land between the trees on the church grounds. Three policemen helped mark the area with the headlights from their squad cars.

Brognola wasted no time on preliminaries. "No planes from Cuba around. Washington National has a couple of 747-SP's on the ground. Korean, I think. There's a Volpar belonging to Courtney Air Freight at Richmond.

"Grimaldi will arrive at Byrd International in a few minutes with the Sabreliner. I doubt you'll need him. I left instructions for the Volpar to be delayed until you got there."

"You expect us all to get in that little thing?" Gadgets asked, pointing at the small Hughes 500-D.

"It's tight, but there's room. And it could land here. Let's go."

Able Team moved toward the chopper. Politician and Gadgets took the back seat. Lao was wedged between Lyons and the pilot on the front bench seat.

The 500-D was a much zippier butterfly than they had expected. It covered the distance of nearly a hundred miles in forty minutes.

Dawn was breaking when they touched down at the Richard E. Byrd International Airport in Richmond, Virginia. The pilot received clearance to land in the freight parking slots. The little chopper touched ground between Stony Man's mat-black Sabreliner and a Volpar-modified, twin-engined Beechcraft.

Although the spinning rotor was almost eight feet from the tarmac, the Able Team members crouched as they ran out under the blades. Each was armed and ready. Jack Grimaldi and a short, wiry, redheaded man walked to meet them.

The freckled redhead raised an eyebrow and asked, "What did I do, drop below assigned altitude again?"

The question and Jack Grimaldi's relaxed slouch brought Able Team up short.

"Like you fellows to meet Courtney, an old flying buddy. Told him you wanted to talk to him," Grimaldi said. He was grinning at the confused look on Carl Lyons's face. It was the first time he'd managed to catch him with a total surprise.

Lyons recovered quickly. "You in El Paso yesterday?"

"Yep."

"Fly anyone out?"

"Nope."

"Anyone see you land in Mexico?"

"Yep."

"Who?"

"Computer type. Signed my invoice and took the computer part I delivered. I'll give you the name and firm if you have to check."

"We check. First name?"

"Don't use one."

Grimaldi laughed. "Drove the air force brass nuts, but they never did find one."

"Okay. Lao, let's put that info through."

"My computer's back in the van. You'll have to radio it back to Stony Man," Lao answered.

Lyons turned to Grimaldi. "You vouch for this guy?"

"With my life. He saved it several times in Nam."

"And you didn't come in under heavy machine gun fire and pull my ass out?" Courtney shot back.

Grimaldi shrugged. "We've done each other some favors," he told Lyons.

The massive understatement bought grins all around.

"Then who the hell got those terrorists off that field?" Gadgets demanded.

"You talking El Paso?" Courtney asked.

"Yeah."

"I can tell you."

"What?"

"I said—"

"Who?" Lyons interrupted.

"I flew straight back to El Paso from Torreón because this flight to Richmond was already booked. The boys at the freight terminal were talking about the manhunt and the airport being cordoned off. Seems like a 747-SP with a big shrimp painted on the tail stalled takeoff. Five men ran out on the field and swarmed up a rope. The plane took off shortly after that."

"Check Washington National," Ironman snapped at Gadgets.

Gadgets moved clear of the buildings to raise Stony Man. He was close to maximum distance for the ultracompact communicators Able Team carried.

"Get the bus ready," Lyons told Grimaldi.

"Hold on," Courtney interrupted. "You owe me."

Lyons paused and raised an eyebrow.

"I've got nothing booked. I want to copilot for Jack. We haven't flown together for years."

"This could turn hot."

"So what?"

"So that means you've got one minute to get ready," Lyons answered. He didn't know why he made an exception for Courtney, but his instincts told him it was the right decision.

Courtney ran for his plane.

Schwarz double-timed it back to the shelter of the hangar. "Guyana Seafood Specialties has a 747-SP in the freight section at Washington International. They just took off. The tower's trying to call them back."

"Fat chance. We'll alert air defense after we take off. Go!" Lyons barked.

Courtney came back from his Volpar, lugging the large briefcase that seemed to come with the job of pilot. Grimaldi already had the port engine whistling to life. Six minutes later they were in the air, heading south.

Politician went forward and took over the plane's radio the moment Jack was through with the control tower and had signed on with the first control area. He squatted behind the pilots' seat for twenty minutes before giving up and going back to report to Lyons.

"Hal's still in flight, so I can't get him. Air defense won't scramble to stop the 747-SP without proof. We can follow if we like, but no one's going to intercept."

"What's Grimaldi say? When do we overtake?"

Politician shook his head. "When hell freezes over. They're traveling about the same as we're managing in this souped-up chariot. The difference is they can keep it up. Grimaldi's got us going close to the red line. He doesn't want to burn out the engines. We're pushing it, they're not. The problem is they can go nonstop. We have to stop to refuel. The only good news is that ground control and radar will tell us where they are all the way home."

"Why didn't Grimaldi have the bird topped up?"

"Calm down, Ironman. He always does, but these oversized engines slurp gas. We have a total fuel capacity of less than thirteen hundred gallons. The big baby we're chasing can drink over fifty thousand gallons at once if it fills up."

Lyons leaned back in silent thought for so long that the rest of Able Team started exchanging puzzled glances. Gadgets finally reached over and pinched Lyons hard enough to make him jump.

"You still with us?"

"See if Grimaldi still has chutes in the aft compartment," Lyons rumbled.

"He isn't going to boot me out without a parachute," Gadgets told the others as he got up. Five seconds later he added, "Yeah. They're here." His voice didn't sound enthusiastic.

Lyons got up and went into the cockpit. In a few seconds the whine of the big Pratt and Whitney engines dropped a few decibels. Lyons came back and sat down before sharing the plan with the rest of the team.

"Jack's slowing down to conserve fuel. He's making arrangements to refuel in Kingston. Then we hop out over the old Rising Sons camp. Grimaldi will double back, land at Port of Spain and arrange for choppers to get us out."

"Oh, great," Gadgets groaned. "Not only do we chase the damn plane a couple of thousand miles, but now Ironman wants to walk home."

"Do you think the Church of the Rising Sons is training ninja killers again?" Lao asked in a quiet voice.

"Don't you?"

She nodded.

"Shit!" Politician breathed. "Karen's there. And a couple of other women and Quincey and a number of kids."

"If you put it that way, we're going in," Gadgets conceded. "Wish we were better equipped."

"We can survive," Lyons snapped. "What's the ammunition situation?"

They took time to count. The situation wasn't great. Lao had six sticks of fifty for her caseless and two spare clips for her .380 Colt Government. Politician had gas grenades for his M-203, two wire-wounds and five phosphorous. He had one spare stick for the M-16 and the mini-Uzi. Gadgets only had the full clip in his .45 MAC-10. He had three spare clips for his Beretta 93-R. Lyons had a twelve-drum of his usual load for the Konzak. He had another drum of slugs, a clip of phosphorous grenades and two clips of lighter shot that would disperse before hitting hostages. He had a spare clip for the Colt and plenty of extra ammo in boxes.

"We can't fight a war," Lyons concluded.

"If you're right, that's what we'll be fighting," Gadgets pointed out.

"Let's plan. Then we get some sleep," Ironman said in a cold voice.

They planned as well as they could with the information available. Then they went to the regular seats and stretched out. Years of living on the edge, fighting terrorism wherever they met it, had ingrained the necessity of grabbing sleep when they could. Necessity conquered battle nerves and excitement.

An hour later Courtney came back to the cockpit from the cabin and told Grimaldi, "Those guys are all dead to the world."

Grimaldi gave his old friend a crooked grin. "I forgot to warn you about that. I'm glad you didn't try to wake them."

"How do you know I didn't?"

"You're in one piece, friend."

Even with clearances and advance arrangements by Stony Man, the Sabreliner was on the ground fourteen minutes for refueling. More time was lost slowing for landing and climbing back to altitude. By the time they were back on course, the 747-SP was circling Georgetown. It had left Washington airspace only four hours and twenty-three minutes earlier.

Ninety minutes later Able Team looked at the jungle three miles below through the open door of the Sabreliner. Courtney had come back to watch the jump, and to close the door behind them.

Normally the jump would have been impossible. The door was just forward of the wing; the body-mounted engine just aft. Anyone jumping would be doomed to hit the engine or the tail plane.

Grimaldi cut the power to the two turbojets and glided toward the target at a hundred and forty miles per hour—the minimum speed before the plane stalled. Able Team stayed poised near the door, tensely waiting.

When he was over target, Grimaldi pulled the flaps down and let the plane stall. The powerless Sabreliner tried to glide in a slightly nose-up position and didn't have the power. It hung in the air for a second and then began to drop as if it had no aerodynamic properties at all.

The moment the plane's forward momentum was lost, Lyons leaped to the doorsill and thrust with his powerful legs. Lao's feet hit the sill the moment Lyons's feet left. Gadgets followed. Politician dove headfirst from two feet back. The team of four had left the plane in three seconds.

Courtney didn't dare leave his seat to shut the door. The plane was sideslipping away from the jumpers, so he couldn't have reached the door anyway. The Sabreliner plummeted toward earth, picking up speed as it went.

With the speed came control. In twenty seconds Grimaldi had it in a dive. Then he leveled the dive to a controlled rate of descent. They were still heading west at a 150 miles per hour.

Courtney could hear the port engine light up as he closed and secured the door. He wondered why it was taking so long to catch. By the time he had returned to the copilot's seat, the engine was thrusting and Jack was beginning to ease them into level flight.

Courtney threw back his head and roared, "Yahoo! This is really living. Sure beats delivering parcels."

Grimaldi grinned as he worked on restarting the starboard engine.

"Glad you're enjoying the cruise. More excitement coming up at twelve o'clock low."

"A Bell 212. Hell! They'll have the entire air force on our tail."

The starboard engine roared, and Grimaldi eased the throttles forward. At the same time he veered and started to climb. Courtney laughed as the Guyanese chopper danced slightly in their wake.

"Let them call out the entire air command," Grimaldi said. "Some cargo transports, three twin-turbo props, six

Islandar STOLs, half a dozen helicopters and a Cessna U-206-F. That's the extent of it.''

"Hope you're right."

"Check the computer. It's all in there," Grimaldi answered as he banked 160 degrees to start for Trinidad.

"What the hell are they doing so far from Georgetown?" Courtney wondered.

"They're having trouble with Venezuela again. They keep troops at the border. The M-212 transports about fourteen fully-equipped troops. Thing's probably stationed in a hamlet right up in the northwest corner of the country, place called Morawhanna.''

"It's a relief to know we're not going to have MiGs dusting our ass," Courtney said. His voice said he was more disappointed than relieved.

THE ABLE TEAM COMMANDOS fell free with their arms and legs spread to slow their fall and to keep from spinning. They all watched the plane slide away from them as Grimaldi fought for control. By the time the engines were ignited and the plane was under power and climbing, it was only a few thousand feet from the rain forest.

They spotted the bow in the Pomeroon and then the camp. As soon as they could see it, Lyons led the way and they soared south of the camp to keep from being seen when they opened their chutes. They were below a thousand feet when Lyons pulled his rip cord. The other terror fighters followed suit.

The landing wasn't an easy one. By trying to stay out of sight of the camp, they found themselves in an area with no clearing. Lao and Politician made it to the ground. Lyons and Gadgets hit trees.

Gadgets knew that he couldn't avoid the tree, so he centered himself on it instead. He crashed through branches, getting scratched in the process. Finally his chute caught, and he was able to release the harness and climb down.

Lyons found himself hanging free, twenty feet above the ground. His solution was unique and typically Ironman. He released his harness with one hand while holding on to the lines with the other. Then he climbed the lines hand over hand and cut three near the shroud. He worked his way down to the end of the cut lines before letting go and dropping a shorter distance to the ground.

The members of Able Team found one another by using a directional facility on their communicators. Politician treated Gadgets's cuts, and they began the trek back to the old Church of the Rising Sons camp.

They moved silently, fanning out, but still in sight of one another.

No one spoke until Gadgets whispered, "We're being followed."

6

Jack Grimaldi landed at Port of Spain, passing the Sabreliner off as a private plane. He arranged for refueling and maintenance, using a company front created by Stony Man to handle such financial transactions. Then he and Courtney checked into the Trinidad Hilton.

The next problem was to get rid of Courtney long enough to make a complete report to Stony Man.

"I've got to call in," he told his old friend. "Find another telephone. Find out if we can rent a chopper that will make the round trip to Guyana and will carry seventeen people."

"You got to be kidding? Who on this island would rent or charter that size of bird?"

"Probably no one, but I can't do anything else until it's checked out."

"Okay," Courtney agreed as he headed for the door of their hotel room, "but she'd better have a friend."

Grimaldi laughed. "Care if the friend's married?"

"Hell, no. Rather have a husband after me than a marriage-hungry female."

"In that case, I know just the person. Just celebrated her diamond anniversary, and she's getting restless."

Courtney's parting shot was, "I'll rent you a chopper with ten gallons of fuel."

When he was alone, Grimaldi pulled a scrambler out of his briefcase and placed a call to Stony Man. Six minutes later Hal Brognola was on the line.

"Where are you?" Brognola snapped. The scrambler device made him sound like a defective robot.

"Port of Spain. Trinidad Hilton. Able Team's in the rain forest in Guyana."

"They're what!"

"They jumped, Hal. They figured the Church of the Rising Sons is back in business and that Quincey and Karen would need their help."

"So you *were* over Guyana. The Guyanese ambassador has already launched protests with the State Department. They're blaming the CIA, of course. He's even called a press conference to denounce CIA interference in the Venezuela-Guyana border dispute."

Grimaldi laughed.

"It's not funny," Brognola snapped. "The CIA's after my ass, and this gives them more ammunition. As far as the government's concerned, Able Team is acting on suspicion only. Now they've made an unauthorized incursion into a foreign country. We're in hot water."

"I'll need a chopper with enough range for the round trip and enough space for seventeen passengers," Grimaldi said.

"No chance. That's military. The President's already involved. I can't tell him we have to make a second illegal incursion. With the press on this, it would be enough to put Able Team permanently out of business."

Jack Grimaldi's tone suddenly grew formal, frigid. It didn't help that he knew the descrambler would lose most of the tone in translation. "I'm sure Able Team wouldn't want those children to be sacrificed as a public relations gesture."

Thinking about the descrambler made Grimaldi sensitive to the pain in Brognola's voice when he said, "The CIA has been trying to get the Team under its wing for two years now. How long would it last then?''

Grimaldi felt like he'd been kicked in the gut. The CIA was as leaky as a sieve. If they had records on Able Team operations, none of the Stony Man warriors would be safe anywhere. He suddenly got the message that Brognola had to pass without putting it into words.

"I'd like to take some of my holiday leave. Port of Spain seems like a pleasant place," Grimaldi said.

There was no mistaking the relief in the head Fed's voice when he said, "Take a few days. We don't need the Sabreliner right away. It would be better on the ground for a while."

Grimaldi hung up and sat deep in thought until Courtney returned twenty minutes later.

"Nothing like that available," Courtney reported.

"That's what I thought," Grimaldi said. His tone of voice made Courtney look at him sharply.

"You sound like your lady friend just told her husband all about you."

Grimaldi didn't grin. He sat in the easy chair by the telephone and stared back at his friend of twenty years. Courtney could sense an internal conflict and sat down without saying anything more. He waited until Grimaldi made up his mind. In typical pilot fashion, Grimaldi thought things through but still came to a rapid decision.

"Our friends have parachuted into political hot water. I'm going to help them, but I'll be on my own. If you were smart, you'd bail out."

Courtney grinned. "Your friends bailed out. Trickiest jump I've ever seen. It seems to have bought them trouble. I think I'd rather ride this one down."

Grimaldi sighed. "Thanks. Now, without going into details, here's the situation: Guyana has lodged a complaint about us with Washington. The organization that the team works for is washing its hands of the situation. I am now a private citizen on leave. We're on our own."

"So we need a way to extract them from a tricky situation and the government couldn't care less. Sounds like Nam all over again. Any suggestions?"

"No. Just procedure. We get them on their radio and see what the hell they need. After that, we make plans to extract them somehow."

Courtney shook his head. "Not good enough. We're the ones who have to tell them they've been written off, right?"

Grimaldi made a face. He knew how much Hal cared, but being written off was essentially correct. It hurt him to make the admission, and it wasn't the first time it had happened either.

Hell! Grimaldi stiffened. He'd just realized that Brognola was behind him one hundred percent. The head Fed had faith that his best pilot could do the job without the might of the United States backing him. He would.

"If you're finished daydreaming," Courtney interrupted, "I was saying that this is going to hit those four cold. It would be better if we had a plan to offer them. Otherwise we're going to be twiddling our thumbs while they're thinking things through."

"I've got the plan," Grimaldi answered, excitement dancing in his eyes.

"You going to let me in on it? Or am I not supposed to know what we're doing?"

After Grimaldi told him, the redheaded pilot shook his head. "No way. You're the one who has to get the Sabreliner out of hock. It eats too much gas for me to foot the bill. The same goes for renting a prop job. You fly. I jump."

"Riskier."

"Not riskier than dealing with a Trinidadian bill collector. You can make the government foot the bills. I can't."

Grimaldi nodded. "Let's go rent a plane."

NO ONE HAD TO ASK Gadgets to check out whoever was following them. Moving silently was his specialty. The other three continued toward the Pomeroon River and the camp started by the Church of the Rising Sons. Gadgets simply vanished behind a growth of roots that grew out and up from a tree.

He crouched and listened. As the sounds of his companions faded, Gadgets could tell that only one person followed. Whoever it was moved very quietly, indicating a familiarity with the forest.

Schwarz suspected that he knew who was tracking them. He faded to the right and moved silently in behind the tracker.

The man was the same height as Lyons but of a smaller build. He wore a dark blue shirt, designer jeans and well-made boots. His uncombed hair was white.

Despite a short struggle with himself, Gadgets couldn't resist the obvious remark. In his normal voice, he said, "Dr. Livingston, I presume."

The figure ahead of him took a nosedive into the nearest bush.

Gadgets took his communicator from his belt, clicked it three times to get the attention of the rest of the team, then said softly, "Double back. Time for a conference."

The Reverend Patrick Henry Quincey got to his feet and brushed himself off. "Schwarz, I don't know whether to kiss you or boot your ass for giving me a heart attack."

"If I have a choice, I'd like to pass on both."

The rest of Able Team filtered back to find Quincey laughing uncontrollably. He waved to acknowledge them and tried to catch his breath. He was laughing more from relief than from Gadgets's remark.

"What did you do to him?" Lao asked.

Lyons spoke before Gadgets could come up with a smart-assed answer. "Is it safe to talk here?"

The question of safety sobered Quincey. He nodded.

"Good to see you fellows. I don't think they've sent patrols this side of the river yet, but we have to be careful. They move quietly."

"Who?"

"Karen's husband showed up with a bunch of mercs in black fatigues. I disappeared into the bush at that point. Figured I was better off loose until I could steal some weapons, but they're careful and highly trained. I thought they might spread out in the forest, hunting me. They didn't make that mistake. Instead, they've got Karen tied to a tree as bait."

"How many?" Lao asked.

"It varies. Down to about thirty right now."

"Men and women?"

"Just men. At first I thought they were Guyanese, but I'm not sure."

"Could they be Muslims?" Lyons asked.

"Arabs? Easily. Did you bring any extra weapons?"

"We arrived light ourselves," Gadgets explained. "Didn't really know we were coming until we got here. You like the MAC-l0, don't you? Use mine, but there's no spare ammo."

He undid the buckles on the thigh clip and passed it to Quincey. The tall man buckled the quick-release mechanism onto his right thigh and checked the weapon. He set the fire selector to semiautomatic before returning the subgun to its holder.

"What now?" he asked Able Team.

"You said they were down to thirty. We should go in tonight before the odds get worse," Lyons decided. "Two hours of recon, then we meet back here to plan."

The five moved out, each in a different direction.

Two hours later they returned. They all had welts from mosquitoes and gnats.

Quincey started the conversation with, "I suppose you saw the reinforcements arrive."

"Was that Yates in command?" Lyons asked.

"Yes."

"Anybody got any ideas?" Lyons wanted to know. When there was no answer, he continued, "I count forty-two in total. The sentries are positioned in several layers on the approach by land and one layer around the edge of the river. They'll let us move in, but they'd keep us from moving out."

The others nodded.

"Gadgets, could you find the sentries in the dark? We'll need to take out a wedge of them along the river. Enough to let us move the kids out without triggering a battle."

"Can do."

"Quincey, can you get the women and kids to cooperate?"

"No problem, but what about Karen?"

"Other women and children first. Either you or Pol may have to try to pass as one of them. Get into the hut and get the kids ready. When we give the signal, we'll take out the window in the back of the building. Everyone goes out that way."

"It'll be watched."

"We'll do something about that. Once we have the kids safe, and a head start on the retreat, we'll try for Karen."

Politician looked at Ironman. Pol's eyes showed the torment he felt. Karen meant a great deal to him. "That means we'll probably abandon her."

"She's a baited trap. We go close, we set off the entire camp. I'll only risk it if it doesn't increase the danger to the kids," Ironman answered, meeting the tormented eyes levelly, coolly.

Pol sighed. "Yeah," he said, but he didn't sound convinced.

"We go in tonight then?" Quincey asked.

Lyons shrugged. "We'll have to wait to hear when the getaway transportation's coming. In the meantime, Quincey, how about supplying some food?"

"You didn't even bring K rations?"

"Didn't know we were coming until Air Command refused to land their plane," Gadgets explained.

The sun was minutes from setting. The group had just managed to quench their thirst on coconut water when Gadgets's communicator buzzed. "News of our taxi service," he announced. After listening for a moment, he told Lyons, "You better deal direct."

Blancanales, Gadgets, Lao and Quincey moved away from Lyons to make sure no one came close enough to hear his voice as he used the radio. He called them back when he was finished.

"We're in shit and Jack's doing what he can," he told the group. "He managed to buy some ammunition and condensed food, but no spare clips, no further weapons and no explosives. He's going to dump Courtney ten to twelve miles up river. We have to find him."

"What's the plan?" Gadgets asked.

"We'll have to ask Courtney. Let's go."

"We have to find one person in the rain forest in the dark? Can't be done," Quincey said.

Lyons grinned. "Grimaldi said to follow the noise."

JACK GRIMALDI WATCHED Courtney's chute slowly fall toward the target area. The large parachute allowed for the extra weight of the supplies.

All the necessities that they could purchase on such short notice were packed in two large dunnage bags that hung from Courtney's harness. It wasn't the safest way to jump, but they couldn't afford the possibility of a supply chute going astray or getting hung up in a tree.

Stony Man's superpilot circled the area once more. He double-checked the horizon. There had been no other planes in sight to see the jump.

It had been a while since Grimaldi had flown anything so light. The Cessna Model 425 Corsair was a light thirty-five-foot plane with twin turboprop engines. It could float along at ninety miles an hour or make time at two hundred and sixty. Jack had to admit to himself that he was enjoying the different feel of the plane.

When he was sure Courtney was going to land by the river, near the stand of balsa they'd spotted, Jack turned the plane east and climbed for height. He went over Georgetown at an altitude of ten thousand feet, knowing they couldn't make out his identification numbers at that height.

He ignored the calls from tower control and flew over. The sun was just setting, and the planes on the field stood out boldly against their own dark shadows. There was no sign of a 747-SP. He thought that was puzzling.

He continued east until he was well over the Atlantic. Then he dived to well below the Georgetown radar and turned north. An hour after that, he climbed back to ten thousand feet and came into Port of Spain from the east.

There was nothing to do now but wait. Worry and wait.

THEIR STOMACHS FORGOTTEN, Able Team and Quincey began to jog up river. Most of the forest was open enough to permit double-timing, but they had to slow occasionally. They were far enough west of the camp that they weren't too concerned about their noise carrying.

Twilight was short. Forty minutes later they had to slow their pace as they moved through the darkness. They headed in a southwest direction for another thirty minutes before reconnecting with the Pomeroon River.

Gadgets led the way, using his small flashlight to spot obstacles and to give the others something to follow.

"We could take all night at this pace and then walk by an entire battalion," Quincey pointed out.

"Listen," Gadgets interrupted.

Everyone paused.

"Don't hear anything but frogs and insects," Lyons said.

Gadgets answered, "Shut up and stay behind me."

They traveled for another half an hour before Pol said, "I hear it now. Sounds like a mechanical mosquito."

"Yeah," Lyons agreed. "What is it?"

"Chain saw," Gadgets told him.

It was easy to find Courtney. He had cut down most of a stand of balsa trees and was trimming them with the chain saw. He worked by the light of a pair of pressure lanterns that gave off an intense white glow. Able Team silently moved into the light.

Courtney looked up without any sense of being startled. "About time you guys got here. I've had to do all the hard work by myself. I'm famished. You willing to make do on camp supplies?"

As they ate a quick meal of dried food and washed it down with coffee, Courtney explained the plan.

"Jack and I pooled our cash. This is what we decided would be most useful under the circumstances—a saw to speed the cutting work, lots of nylon rope, ammo but no magazines and a few days supply of food. Be careful with those pots. If we lose them, the food's almost useless. And, of course, I've got iodine tabs for the water."

"Tastes hideous," Gadgets said.

"But safe. Let's get to work. We've got rafts to finish."

"Let's do this once more," Lyons said. "The plan is to make rafts, pull the kids out and go downriver to the coast."

"We figure it would be the easiest way to move kids. You don't leave tracks, and the kids don't have to walk."

"What do we do on the coast?"

"Get to Morawhanna. You've got a job to do, then I fly you to Port of Spain by helicopter."

"What's our job?" Pol asked.

Courtney grinned. "You fellows have to take the helicopter from the military and fuel it up."

Blancanales couldn't believe his ears. "With children along, we have to go against the Guyanese Army?"

Courtney laughed out loud. "Jack said it was a piece of cake for you guys."

Politician turned to Lyons. "What do we do?"

Lyons stood up. "Whatever the man says. He's the raft builder."

7

The balsa trees Courtney had cut ranged from four to eight inches in diameter. He'd used the chain saw to trim the few branches on the smooth, straight logs. Under Courtney's direction the group notched the logs so that they could be tied together in a three-layer cross lattice.

"These logs are so light we could get by on one or two layers," Quincey observed.

"Not without risking hypothermia," Courtney answered. "That river is fine for swimming across, but if the kids spend the day with cold water washing over their legs, we're asking for trouble. Three layers should hold an adult and three children well above the water."

"What about the sun?"

"Use the thinner tops of the trees for a pole framework. I brought plastic sheeting for roofing," Courtney told him.

Quincey, who considered himself somewhat of a survival expert, admitted, "You seem to know what you're talking about."

"They stuck me on pilot survival training before I finally managed to get posted to Nam."

With six of them working and Courtney's head start on log cutting, raft production sped ahead. They had six roofed rafts finished in under an hour.

Courtney cut two long poles for each raft. He lashed a spare to each framework and handed the rest around. "My job's done until you get us to Morawhanna," he told Lyons.

"Lash the rafts together, two wide, three long," Lyons ordered. "We don't want to get separated in the dark, and joining them will make them harder to tip. One man to a raft. Use the poles to keep to the center of the stream. Make sure you have your spare ammunition before we push off."

Ten minutes later the lamps were extinguished and left behind. So was the saw, which had little gas left.

It took a while to learn to keep the rafts to the center of the stream. When that was mastered, Lyons laid out his battle strategy.

"We pull up at the closest point to the Quonset. Gadgets and Lao clear a wedge of guards up to the back of the hut. Then Quincey and Lao go in for the kids while we hold the wedge open. Keep it quiet, if you can. We can't afford a shoot-out. We'll move the two women and the kids quietly to the rafts. Then we'll see whether we can get Karen. We'll move the kids beyond the fire zone before we try. She's a fuse in a powder keg."

The plan was greeted with silence. No one wanted to risk leaving a friend behind, but they all knew the children had to be freed first.

The jungle night surrounded them. Insects droned, tree frogs chirped and somewhere along the bank, a caiman launched itself into the water.

The current carried them back toward the terrorist camp at a respectable speed, but it was 0230 hours before Lyons whispered the order for them to pole for shore.

Gadgets and Lao leaped off the rafts and vanished without a sound. Quincey stepped off next and used a length of rope to tie the group of rafts to the base of the small tree. Lyons and Blancanales then stepped to firm ground and crouched quietly, listening. Courtney held his position. He was to help settle people onto the rafts.

Gadgets was the first to encounter a guard. The man was standing with his back to a tree only twenty yards down-

stream from where the rafts were tied up. He watched the
river for swimmers. If Ironman had missed the landmarks
in the light of the quarter moon, the rafts would have drifted
right past the motionless guard. He couldn't have failed to
see them.

The rafts sloshed slightly when someone stepped off,
causing the ninja-trained Arab to jerk his head in that
direction. Gadgets caught the sudden motion and froze.

The black form glided noiselessly toward the change in
river sounds, confident of his own invisibility. An equally
quiet form rose from the ground directly ahead of him. Before the ninja could react, a mat-finished knife plunged into
his larynx. He died silently, quickly. Gadgets caught the
crumpling form and lowered it slowly to the ground.

Gadgets reclaimed his knife before doing anything else.
A quick search of the body yielded another fighting knife
and an automatic, but no spare ammo. Gadgets scouted the
immediate area before taking the time to quietly roll the
body into the river. He didn't want a relief or guard captain
to trip across a dead guard.

It took Lao a few minutes to make sure there were no
guards upriver from the rafts. She then checked a sweep of
bush forty feet inland from the raft position. Still no one.
She passed Gadgets and began to sweep the bush fringe between the river and the clearing for more guards.

Lao's sweep was slow and careful, but despite that, she
and the second guard discovered each other at the same
time.

Lao reacted while the guard was still attempting to identify whether she was friend or foe. Her small fist, one
knuckle extended, connected with the large man's temple.
There was a small cracking noise that wouldn't carry more
than a few yards. The terrorist collapsed.

Lao eased him to the ground and made sure there was no
pulse before searching him. She retrieved two sharp *shuri-*

ken and an automatic without spare ammunition. She put the *shuriken* into a pocket and went back for Lyons.

Gadgets found a third guard another twenty feet beyond the body left by Lao. The man was seated on a stump, stealing a few drags on a cigarette. The glow was a beacon, telling the Stony Man warrior that the guard was confident no one else was in the vicinity.

Gadgets rose to his feet behind his target and gently cleared his throat. The man tried to crush his butt as he pivoted his head. Gadgets grabbed the jaw in his right hand and the back of the neck with his left. He continued the head-turning motion with a violence that snapped the spine, then lowered the body to the ground.

He relieved the dead guard of another Stechin and a garrote. He returned to the body Lao had left in time to meet Lao and Lyons. Blancanales would hold the far perimeter. Lyons would hold from this side.

Lyons pocketed the two spare automatics. Then he and Gadgets carried the two bodies to the river. It was a slow job, testing each footstep to ensure silence.

With their flanks guarded, Gadgets led Lao and Quincey toward the back of the Quonset. The window was small and covered with both wire mesh and a screen. The only other way in was through the door. Gadgets indicated that Quincey should hold position while he scouted in one direction and Lao in the other.

Time was ticking by. Able Team had to get the children downriver before there was enough light to enable the terrorists to follow the rafts.

Gadgets crawled along the side of the Quonset, looking for guards. There were none he could detect. He saw Karen slouched against the tree. He knew that guards would be watching her, but he couldn't spot them. He didn't have time to outwait them. The problem had to be solved from the back.

Gadgets returned to the back of the Quonset and examined the mesh with his fingers. It was screwed in place. He fished for his emergency tools and produced a flat-handled screwdriver. It took a great deal of nerve-stretching work to take the screws out and cut the screen.

The window inside was already open. It and another small window on the opposite wall were the only sources of air for the hut. Lao let herself inside, followed by Quincey. Gadgets held the position by the open window, ready to help people escape.

It was much darker inside the hut.

Quincey whispered in Lao's ear, "How do we wake these people without rousing the entire camp?"

"We have to be careful, but noise in here will be considered natural," she answered.

She groped her way on her hands and knees until she found someone sleeping on the floor. Her quick touch told her it was a child. She continued, checking people by touch. The third child she touched was awake.

"Who's that?" he asked in a curious voice.

"A friend," Lao told him. "Call someone to come and talk to us."

"Mrs. Johnson," the boy called.

"Who's that?" a sleepy voice said.

"Andrew. Someone's here."

When she heard Johnson stirring, Lao retreated, leaving Quincey closest to the child. There was the scratch of a match on the rough side of a matchbox, and the flame of a candle lit the hut.

Norma Johnson looked up and gasped. "Reverend Quincey!"

"Shhh," he answered. "You've got to come with me. We can't risk any noise."

Their voices woke another child and Lisa Frane. The child sat up groggily, rubbing his eyes, and looked at Quincey's tall form. Frane snapped to a sitting position, alarm and a trace of panic putting her on full alert.

"What are you doing here?" she gasped.

"I've come to get you out of this," Quincey said.

"You'll endanger the children." Frane's voice rose in volume. She paused and drew in a lungful of air.

Lao, ignored to this point, made her presence known. Her hand flashed, and the edge caught Frane at the back of the skull, knocking her unconscious.

"What did you do that for?" Quincey demanded. He had once had his doubts about Frane's loyalty, but because he had no proof he'd kept quiet. She had done nothing else to arouse his suspicions.

"She might have shouted," Lao answered.

The children knew Quincey, and they all seemed relieved to see him. It took just a few whispers about going home, if they didn't make a sound, to have them quietly slipping into their clothing.

Norma Johnson and Lao were dressing Frane's unconscious form when someone pounded on the door. Johnson sprang to the door and opened it a crack before either Quincey or Lao could stop her. "Quiet," she demanded in a hoarse whisper. "You'll wake the rest of the children."

"What's going on in there?" a voice whispered back.

"Bad dreams."

"Put the light out."

"Soon."

She shut the door and leaned against it, gathering back her strength and nerve.

Within minutes the children were grouped near the back window and the candle was blown out. Lao slid out the window first. Then Quincey handed out the children one at a time, and either Gadgets or Lao carried them quietly to Courtney, who settled them on the rafts.

Norma Johnson had trouble getting through the small window, but she made no sound. She moved slowly but quietly when Lao took her by the hand to guide her to the rafts.

Frane groaned once as she was passed out to Gadgets. He carried her over his shoulder to the river. Tall and lanky, Quincey had no trouble hoisting himself through the small window to follow Gadgets to the shore.

After Gadgets dumped Frane on board and motioned for Courtney to keep her quiet, he and Lao went to report their progress to Lyons. The operation had taken just under an hour from the time they had tied up near the camp. Dawn was less than two hours away.

Lyons nodded, indicating they were to do what they could to free Karen. He didn't need to tell them that if the camp was aroused, their chances of survival were slim.

Gadgets moved from shadow to shadow, studying the open area for ten minutes before coming up with a plan. He crawled back and conferred with Lao.

She crawled to the Quonset hut and back in through the window. She then used the butt of her H&K G-11 to tap out a soft, steady beat against the metal side of the hut.

Gadgets lay in the weeds near the clearing until he saw two figures move from the shadows toward the door of the hut. He left the shadows and walked silently behind them as if he too were going to investigate the noise. But he moved in a long arc that took him past the tree.

As Gadgets passed Karen, he paused. Under the guise of checking her bonds, he sliced through the ropes that held her wrists. Then he waved a loose end of rope angrily at the branches above him.

As a figure dropped quietly from the tree, Gadgets bent down and sliced the ropes holding Karen's feet. Then he gestured for the man who had been hiding in the tree to look at the cut ropes.

When the man bent over, a mat-finished Gerber slashed across the front of his throat. The terrorist tried to stop the flow of blood with his hands, but he couldn't.

Gadgets took Karen's hand to lead her away. She looked at him through glassy eyes, took a step and collapsed.

Lao kept up her steady rhythm of tapping against the metal wall until a fist pounded on the door. She opened the door, then stepped back into the shadows. The two men outside paused for a few beats, then entered.

The second one through the door had his head nearly removed by the swinging butt of Lao's G-11. He dropped in the doorway.

The first one spun into a defensive position. His timing was perfectly matched to Lao's. The barrel of the H&K caseless rammed into his solar plexus hard enough to knock the wind from him. He crashed to the floor and writhed until his temple was crushed by another blow from the assault rifle.

And then another ninja leaped to the door and shouted the alarm.

8

When the alarm sounded, Lao decided to try to hold the Quonset as long as possible to give the rest time to get away.

She punched the shouting terrorist through the door with three slugs in his chest. Then she threw herself to the floor near the back of the building. She stayed close to the open window, but couldn't be hit if someone fired in at her. She lay with her G-11 covering the open door at the front.

Gadgets heard the three-shot voice of Lao's caseless and knew things had gone sour. He lifted Karen onto his left shoulder and ran back the way he'd come, his heart pounding. His silenced Beretta 93-R filled his right fist. If a bullet struck Karen, he didn't want to be the one to tell Politician.

Politician and Lyons had reacted to the firing by closing in to cover the rafts. Gadgets lowered Karen onto a raft near the shore and left her under Courtney's care.

"Go," Lyons ordered. "We'll meet the rafts on the north side of the camp."

The rafts were untied and moved gently with the current. Courtney and Quincey sat nearest the action. Each had a pole in one hand and a weapon in the other.

The three Able Team warriors moved cautiously to the back of the Quonset, arriving at the same time as three black-clad figures. In the predawn darkness, only Gadgets's ears could pick out the soft footfalls of the ninja-trained enemy. He would grab one of his teammates and point him in the right direction.

Three Arab assassins discovered the open window at about the same time. Before they could decide on a course of action, three other silent figures moved in behind them.

Lyons simply wrapped a long arm around his target's neck. One sudden jerk of the arm and the man's neck broke with a small snap.

Blancanales swung the barrel of his assault rifle into the temple of the next man. Shards of bone were driven into the brain, dispatching him to Allah on the trash express.

Gadgets's silenced Beretta cleared its throat once. The lead entered at the base of the terrorist's neck and exploded out his forehead, taking mashed brain with it.

"The back is clear," Politician said in the window. His voice was drowned out by a subgun that sent a spray of lead through the thin metal walls of the Quonset.

The terrorists didn't know yet that their prisoners had escaped. They were operating on the assumption that one person inside had a gun. The spray of fire announced that they didn't care how many innocent children died as long as they got their target.

Politician called again, and Lao dived out the window just as another spray of fire went through the walls from another angle.

"You shouldn't have held up the raft," Lao said to them.

"We didn't. We supply a diversion, then catch up," Lyons answered.

They picked up two automatics and a PPSh-41 from the three corpses, then went around the corner of the Quonset, blasting terrorists with their own Russian-supplied weapons.

"North to the place where the river bends near the trail again," Lyons ordered above the din. "We pick up the rafts there."

"That's about two miles in the dark," Gadgets protested.

"Better idea?" Lyons demanded.

"No. Let's haul ass."

The captured weapons were empty, and the entire camp was awake and entering the battle. As each weapon clicked empty, it was tossed aside.

Able Team fought their way through the perimeter on the land side and found the rutted trail. They stopped firing and started running as fast as they could over the uneven terrain in the dark.

They could hear the sound of a truck being started back at the camp.

"We need a narrow place to stop the first truck," Lyons commanded. "Find a place where they can't get the other vehicles by."

The could hear the whine of the low gear as the truck took to the trail behind them. Soon it would catch up and pick them out with its headlights.

Gadgets's radio clicked five times, but he didn't have the time or the breath to answer it.

"This will have to do," Blancanales shouted.

They were at the spot where the trail had been hacked through a stand of palm trees. The trees, crowding in on either side, would prevent other trucks from going around a stopped vehicle.

"Fire phosphorous grenades into the back of the truck," Lyons ordered Politician.

Lyons slid the drum out of his Konzak and put in a six-pack of slugs.

Gadgets had only his Beretta. Not being part of the action, he turned his attention to his communicator. He clicked it three times.

"Gadgets?"

"Right on, Courtney. You got Grimaldi's radio?"

"Yeah. We're holding up two hundred yards past the camp. Went by without incident."

"Keep going. We'll meet you two miles from the camp. Don't wait for us. Whatever you do, keep moving."

"Read you."

The truck swept around the bend. Lyons's assault shotgun roared six times on semiauto. The first three shots went through the bulletproof windshield, leaving three equally spaced holes across the driver's side. The next three shots drilled through the front of the radiator.

Politician overshot his first phosphorous grenade. It sailed through the soldiers in the back of the truck and exploded two feet beyond the tailgate. Two terrorists screamed as the burning particles hit their legs.

His next shot arced over the back of the truck, exploding over the heads of the murderers. There was a great deal of screaming and thrashing as the particles burned their way into human flesh.

Able Team took to the trail again. Running away from the truck's headlights, their eyes slowly adjusted to the darkness of the forest. They could hear another truck come to a stop behind the first. Soon there would be soldiers on foot behind them.

The terrain was so treacherous that each commando fell once or twice. It was better to fall than to try to maintain balance and twist an ankle.

"It will be dawn soon," Lyons told them. "Keep moving."

Although the Pomeroon's current moved faster than Able Team could in the dark, the river meandered. They had a good chance of reaching their intercept point before the rafts. They had no idea how well the killers behind them were doing. The only safe assumption was that they could move at least as quickly as Able Team.

The long stretch of watching, traveling to meet Courtney, raft building and fighting was beginning to show. Their footsteps slowed, and their breathing was ragged.

"Here," Lyons said. "Veer left. Keep it quiet."

Able Team came to a stop, breathing hard. Then they moved in the general direction of the river. It was even more difficult to run through the dense trees, roots and vines than it had been on the broken trail.

They heard no sound of pursuit, but that meant nothing. The terrorists had been trained to move quietly, and they could easily be right behind.

The sun was beginning to rise before they found the river. There was no sign of the enemy, but no one relaxed his guard. Gadgets spoke in a low voice when he tried his radio. He clicked the transmit button several times.

"Courtney here." When the voice came, it was close, loud.

"We're at the river. You sound close," Gadgets said. "The problem is whether you're ahead of us or behind us."

"What if I shout?"

"The enemy is tailing us."

"Not a good idea then."

There was a moment's silence, then Gadgets said, "Keep going. We'll hold position. If the signal fades, you're ahead of us. If not, you'll find us."

"It will be tough on you if we're ahead. We've been making good time."

"We'll have to take the chance. Don't slow down. We can't let the children be recaptured."

"Ten-four," Courtney answered.

"Movement at four o'clock," Gadgets whispered ten minutes later.

"Investigate," Ironman whispered back. "We can't afford noise at this stage."

Gadgets went down on his belly and crawled toward the sound. As he approached, it seemed to cover a wider area. He stopped, confused. Then he realized that some of the sound came from directly above him. Slowly he rolled onto his back. Nearly a dozen pair of eyes stared down at him

Gadgets cursed his luck and rolled once more onto his stomach. A huge beetle strolled slowly across his left hand He waited tensely until it was off him, then began his slow and cautious crawl back toward the group.

After traveling forty feet, he rolled and looked up once more. He let out a sigh of relief. They weren't following. He continued to move away at a crawl.

When Gadgets reached the place where he'd left his companions, there was no sign of them.

He searched for a sign and soon found some flattened plants. The trail led the final dozen feet to the river. Gadgets crawled the rest of the way.

He spotted the lashed-together rafts on the river. The rest of Able Team was tensely watching the jungle and holding on to the rafts. When they saw that Gadgets was still crawling, they grew tenser.

Gadgets moved quietly to the rafts and rolled onto one He spoke in a soft voice. "Just move quietly and get us out of here."

Lao, Politician and Ironman stepped on board. Quincey on one end and Courtney on the other poled them out into the current. They were soon sweeping downstream. Gadgets looked up at the curious glances of the children and marveled at how silent they were.

"We're having a quiet contest," Politician explained "The one who is quiet the longest gets to be first off the plane when we reach the good old U.S. of A. What was it you saw?"

"Spider monkeys," Gadgets told him. "They were huddled in the tops of trees in clusters of three and four. Just waking up, I guess. They saw me but just watched. I didn't want to disturb them any more than I had to. If they started to scream or throw things, everyone for miles around would have known exactly where we were.''

"Congratulations," Quincey said from the front of the rafts. "I didn't know you were such a naturalist."

"I'm not. But those monkeys almost cost us a few lives in Central America. I'm not about to forget them in a hurry."

Able Team ate some emergency rations and passed the chocolate bars to the children. Gadgets offered some of the food to a thin woman with long black hair. She ignored the offer.

Quincey laughed and said, "Gadgets, meet Lisa Frane. She's the unconscious woman you carried to the raft. Lao knocked her out when we went for the children. Lisa hasn't been sociable since coming to. I don't think she thinks we're going to make it."

Norma Johnson sipped water but passed up all offers of food, saying it should go to the children.

Karen contented herself with small sips of water to relieve her long spell of dehydration. She glared at Quincey from time to time but said nothing.

"How you doing?" Quincey asked her.

"You didn't care enough to hang around when George came. Why pretend you care now?" she said to him in a quiet voice.

"Hold it," Politician said. "Don't tell me you're angry at Pat for slipping into the jungle?"

"Why should that make me mad? I adore cowards."

Quincey made no attempt to reply. He devoted his energy to keeping the rafts in midstream.

"That's not fair," Blancanales said in a mild voice. "His action might have been what saved everyone's lives."

Karen gave him a puzzled look.

"There was less chance of a murder if someone was loose who might report it. His being free was your insurance. He was the one taking the real risks."

Karen said nothing, but she stared at the jeanclad minister. He pretended to be too busy to overhear the conversation that was taking place right in front of him.

Before the situation could become any tenser, Lyons butted in. "I want everyone to eat."

"I couldn't," Johnson protested. "I'd be sick."

"We could deal with that, but if you get weak from hunger, we'll have a problem."

He pulled his last bottle of Gatorade from his pack, opened it and passed it to Karen.

"Sip this, sparingly." There was no mistaking the command in his voice.

Karen made a face but took small mouthfuls of the sweet liquid.

The sun rose over the trees and pounded down on the river. From time to time, Courtney and Quincey passed around river water treated with iodine tablets. It tasted terrible, but Able Team drank large quantities and bullied the women and children into taking enough to prevent dehydration.

They began to pass small settlements of round native houses built mostly of bamboo and thatched leaves. A few canoes passed them on the river, the paddlers staring openly and smiling as they returned the children's waves.

It was evening when they left the rafts and walked over a high ridge to an ocean town called Charity. The town had twelve hundred people and an open-air market.

Lyons stopped the group and had them sit and rest on the southern slope, back far enough from the ridge to avoid drawing attention to themselves. He studied the town from a distance before sending Quincey ahead to buy Able Team clothing. There was no way they'd get along the coast looking like troops on the move.

An hour later Quincey came back with pants and shirts that were a reasonable fit but poorly made. Lyons had to be content with overalls since there was nothing large enough for him in the market stalls.

"Good thing you were cautious," Quincey told Lyons. "There are eight Guyanese soldiers watching the mouth of the river."

Lyons grunted. He expected it. The Guyanese government wouldn't be anxious to have them return to the United States with stories of terrorists hiding in the rain forest.

"The big problem is that I couldn't find a thing to carry the weapons in. There's a boat due in the morning. I bought some food, beer and lots of pop," Quincey reported.

"Let's make camp. I'll think of something," Lyons said.

They moved southeast to a level place to camp and started a fire.

After the exhausted children had eaten and were asleep on the ground, Quincey completed his report to the adults. "Technically we're supposed to have permits to travel outside the capital. Our group had papers, but not to travel to Morawhanna. If someone asks us for our travel permits, we're up the creek. Our only hope is that no one will ask to see them. Someone on the packet that goes along the coast will probably ask. And there's apt to be more soldiers on that stretch." Quincey finished by asking, "Where's Lisa? I haven't seen her for half an hour."

"It's okay," Gadgets told him. "Lao went to find her. I hear them now."

Frane stormed out of the bush followed closely by Lao.

"She got lost," Lao said.

Frane glared at her but said nothing.

Lyons heaved himself to his feet. Unshaven, his fatigue top stained with salt from sweat, his boots muddy, he looked like a farmer who'd just purchased his first new jeans in three years.

"I'm going into town. Politician, come along. The rest of you take it easy."

Quincey watched Politician and Ironman stride off along a path that ran parallel to the river.

"No one's going to trust a pair of bums like that," he muttered.

"Wanna bet?" Gadgets asked.

Quincey shook his head.

It was after dark when Lyons and Pol returned. They carried something bulky between them. Gadgets had drawn the first watch. He chuckled when he saw what they carried.

Dawn found Lyons on watch, sitting on the coffin he and Blancanales had carried into camp the night before.

When Courtney raised an eyebrow, Politician explained, "Poor Aunt Mildred. We're taking her back to Morawhanna to bury her. We figure Aunty weighted only ninety pounds."

After a breakfast of hot soup, bread and jam, they carried the coffin solemnly into town and proceeded straight to the pier. The soldiers must have camped at the mouth of the river, farther west. There was no sign of them.

The pier was a wide board affair that had enough room for larger crowds than the coastal packets could possibly carry. The police station was a two-story building right on the pier. It was the only building in the entire community that was freshly painted.

The market had taken over most of the pier. There were stalls everywhere, even along the front of the police station. The vendors' only concession to authority was a four-foot gap between the stalls that allowed the police access to their building.

Able Team kept their eyes peeled, but the only sign of police activity was a tired-looking man in shorts who carefully carried two Styrofoam cups of coffee from a dilapidated stall into the station.

The seventy-foot coastal packet looked amazingly shipshape when it pulled in about eight. Its white paint was fresh, and it wasn't more than ten years old. While plantains were off-loaded, Able Team and their charges went aboard with ten other passengers.

Politician didn't wait for sailing time to deal with the problem of their lack of papers. He sought out the captain, a stout man of about fifty, who was checking manifests with the supercargo.

"Captain?"

The seaman looked over Politician's scruffy appearance before acknowledging his position.

"We have a problem."

"If you lack funds—"

Politician smiled. "If I needed a loan, I'd talk to my banker. I have wet travel documents. Can we go to your cabin where I can spread them out without tearing them? There's also the question of the extra freight for taking along the...ah..." Politician let his voice trail off as he gestured toward the coffin.

Very few men are slow-witted when it comes to talking money. Politician had made it obvious that he had money and wished to discuss money matters in private. The captain of the vessel needed no further clues. He finished what he was doing, then led Blancanales to a small cabin that was used as an office.

As soon as the door was closed, Pol pulled his roll of bills from his pocket. The roll was still wet from the previous day's swim back and forth across the river.

"There are nine adults in our party," Politician told the captain. As he spoke, he counted nine twenties onto the desk. "And nine children." Nine tens followed the twenties. "And a coffin. Aunty wanted to be buried in her hometown." A fifty went on top of the pile. "I trust our travel papers are in order."

The captain made no move toward the money, then he said, "The purser collects the fares."

"We'll be happy to pay him. I merely wanted you to check our travel papers. We're strangers in your country and want to make sure they're all right."

The $320 in American bills disappeared.

"You realize there's an army encampment on the outskirts of Morawhanna?"

"I didn't know, but I doubt if they'll attend the service."

The captain shrugged. "I hope you have a pleasant voyage," he said, leading the way out of the office.

They arrived in Morawhanna by lunchtime. It was a town of three hundred with a temporary encampment of a hundred and fifty soldiers on the outskirts. The roads were little more than mud pathways, and the houses were hastily constructed shacks. A small store, rather than a market, served the population.

"There's our helicopter!" Courtney exclaimed in an excited whisper.

"Great!" Gadgets said. "Now all we have to do is figure how to steal it from the center of a military camp."

The Bell M-212 sat in a circle of baked mud. The army tents surrounded it.

9

"Sooner or later the army is going to be told to check out everyone traveling with kids. We have to move before then," Lyons told the group.

They sat around an evening fire. Morawhanna's few lights were a dim glow to the northwest.

"Even if we could capture and hold the chopper, we can't board the women and children in the middle of a firefight," Quincey said.

"No firefights," Lyons insisted. "This government's supposed to be friendly, even if they are hiding Khaddafi's assassins."

"Then how?"

"We'll have to liberate some uniforms and borrow the thing from under their noses. Courtney's the problem," Blancanales answered.

"Me? Why am I a problem?"

"You wouldn't believe how few Guyanese have red hair and freckles," Gadgets said in a dry voice. "We'll have trouble passing you off as one of their own pilots."

"Sorry. My parents didn't know you'd have those requirements."

Lyons ignored the small talk and kept working on the problem, saying, "We want those uniforms tonight. When's the best time to leave?"

"Half an hour after dawn," Politician replied. He was the team's operations specialist. They listened when he decided the best time for an action.

"Why not earlier, when there's less light to count freckles by?" Courtney asked.

"Everyone knows 0300 to 0400 is supposed to be the lax time for sentries," Blancanales explained. "If we go in then, the timing will seem suspicious. We'd be expected to hang around and leave by daylight. If we go in earlier, the idea of a night flight will have them radioing all over the place. Let's get them up about an hour before they'd normally be stirring. Too late to go back to bed and too early to think about anything except getting some coffee. There'll be no excuse for not leaving as soon as the chopper's fueled."

"What makes you think it isn't serviced and ready to go?" Courtney asked.

"It could be, but I'll bet they put off servicing until today."

"Point taken."

"Gadgets, you and Pol are the only two who can pass in a Guyanese uniform. You two do the shopping," Lyons commanded.

Gadgets nodded.

"It's just after ten. Should be prank time," Politician said.

Gadgets grinned and picked up a piece of rope. "Let's go have fun," he told Pol.

The two warriors put on their night camous and faded into the night.

"The women get the first watch and you get the second," Lyons told Quincey. "Everyone has to be up before dawn. We need to find a landing place as early as possible."

A TEMPORARY BIVOUAC always seems to bring out the schoolboy in a group of soldiers. The two-week-old camp near Morawhanna was no exception. Captain David Lord was wakened to the sound of cursing from the next tent. He slid on his shirt and pants, jammed his feet into unlaced boots and went to investigate.

Lord was a heavyset man who stood five-eleven in his bare feet.

The adjacent tent had collapsed. The men were crawling out from under the canvas, with only their tempers worse for wear. A sentry and a burly sergeant were already on the scene.

Captain Lord was within six feet before they recognized him and saluted.

"What happened, Sergeant?"

"Jokers," Sergeant Givens said with distaste. "First a sentry is tripped with a rope. Then the guy ropes for this tent were cut."

"We'll make an example of the culprits, Sergeant. This nonsense has to stop. Border patrol is serious business."

"Yes, sir."

The sergeant was saved further speeches by angry shouts from another part of the camp. They ran in that direction to find another tent down.

Before Captain Lord could organize anything, a voice barked, "Captain Lord, what's happening?"

With a sigh of resignation the captain turned in time to have the beam from the colonel's flashlight shine into his eyes.

"Pranksters, sir."

"You're O.T.D. Get them."

"Yes, sir."

When the colonel had gone back to his cot, Lord told Sergeant Givens, "We're up. We've just volunteered. We'll patrol the camp quietly until we find which unit's sneaking out of its tent.''

"Yes, sir,'' Givens replied wearily.

From his hiding place in a clump of trees on one side of the camp, Gadgets whispered into his communicator, "Bingo.''

"Where?'' Blancanales's voice came back.

"The two walking around the tents seem to be our sizes. One's wearing an officer's cap.''

"Who carries?''

"My idea. You carry.''

"Uh-uh. Your idea. You carry it through.''

"One each.''

"Okay, but you first.''

Gadgets moved into the camp, passing within fifteen feet of a sentry who was more interested in trying to spot the practical jokers than he was in watching outside the perimeter. When Gadgets had a tent between himself and the sentry, he waited. He heard the unnatural rustle of a bush just outside the perimeter of the camp.

"Who goes?'' the sentry demanded.

Gadgets mentally thanked Politician for his timely distraction and eased his way deeper into the camp. He saw the bareheaded target standing ahead of him, but passed the man up. He prowled until he was lying next to a tent being approached by the target wearing the officer's cap.

He lay still in the shadow of the tent until the officer strolled past. The man looked directly toward Gadgets but failed to see him.

Gadgets moved silently behind the officer and chopped the back of his neck. The target collapsed without uttering a sound. Gadgets picked up the cap and put it on his own head. Then he dragged the unconscious man into the deeper shadows between tents, stripped him and put on his uniform.

When he was ready, he used his communicator to tell Politician, "Now."

Gadgets then bent down and hoisted the unconscious man to his shoulder and walked calmly back toward the small clump of trees.

From the other side of the camp, a voice shouted, "Stop or I'll shoot."

Immediately after came the sound of three shots.

Gadgets walked from the camp while all eyes strained toward the far edge. Unfortunately the guard wasn't distracted a second time.

"Who goes there?" he challenged.

"Caught one," Gadgets told him.

The guard advanced to see who it was. His curiosity bought him a kick to the gut that knocked his wind out before he could speak.

Gadgets had to drop his burden and finish knocking out the guard. He then found himself dragging two bodies into the bush. He had to crawl while he dragged the second, because most of the camp was up now.

When Politician showed up ten minutes later, the two captives were bound and gagged.

"Did you have to start shooting?" Gadgets complained. "It's going to be tougher to get your uniform."

"I didn't. The guards on the other side of camp have itchy trigger fingers. They shot at the bush I rattled. Luckily they're poor shots."

"How do we get your uniform now?" Gadgets moaned.

Pol's teeth caught a bit of moonlight when he grinned.

"You're the captain. Order me one."

Gadgets sighed and headed back toward the camp. This time the missing sentry made it possible for him to penetrate the perimeter before he was spotted.

"Who's there?" a sentry on his left challenged.

"Shut up," Gadgets snapped back. Then he pointed at the bulky NCO who still roamed among the tents. "Get him over here, quietly."

The sentry ran to do as commanded. A minute later, Gadgets could make out the sergeant's stripes on the big man's sleeve. Before the sergeant could recognize the imposter, Gadgets turned his back and pointed outward. Puzzled, the sergeant approached.

"What is it, sir?"

Gadgets dropped his left hand and said in a soft voice, "It's a Beretta 93-R. It's silenced. If you don't do exactly as I say, it goes off."

He held his Beretta just far enough from his body to let the sergeant see it.

Gadgets continued speaking, "If you do as I say, no one gets hurt."

"I don't believe you." The Guyanese soldier's voice was flat, hard, but pitched low.

"The sentry got in my way, but he's still alive. Will seeing him convince you?"

There was a long pause. "What do you want?"

"I need your uniform. Before we take off in the helicopter we'll release the three of you."

"Then you have Captain Lord, too."

Nothing wrong with the sergeant's brain. He was cool.

"Yes."

"Alive?" The sergeant still kept his voice low.

"Yes."

"He'll blame me for this. Get rid of him and I'll cooperate."

"Forget it."

The sergeant shrugged and walked ahead, keeping his hands at his side, but in sight. Gadgets directed him toward a clump of bushes. When he bent down in the bad light and recognized Captain Lord, his breath escaped in an audible release of tension.

"It's a hard shot to call," Gadgets said to Politician in a soft voice. "Pick up one of the men. We have a long way to walk."

"What about the other one?" Pol asked.

"You got to do something. I'm keeping the prisoner covered."

Quincey was on guard duty by the time Gadgets and Blancanales got back with their three prisoners. They tied and gagged all three and left them under Quincey's care. The two Able Team warriors grabbed ninety minutes of sleep.

At dawn Politician and Gadgets dressed in their borrowed uniforms. They waited until Courtney finished his coffee, then tied his hands behind him. Politician took the guard's rifle, and Gadgets tucked his unsilenced Beretta into his newly acquired Sam Browne belt. They started back toward the army bivouac.

The rest of the group moved east along the coast until they found a level spot for the helicopter to land. They marched the prisoners ahead of them.

It was 0415 when a nervous sentry stopped Blancanales, Gadgets and Courtney on the edge of the Guyanese Army bivouac.

"Captain Forbes with a prisoner. Call the officer of the day," Gadgets said.

He returned the sloppy salute and waited while another sentry was dispatched. The sentry returned ten minutes later.

"Captain Lord isn't in his tent. I can't find him."

"Then get the commander. I'm in a hurry," Gadgets snapped.

It wasn't an errand the second guard did willingly, but he went. Ten minutes later he returned following a colonel in a rumpled uniform. The man looked almost as unshaven as Politician and Gadgets.

"Captain Forbes, sir," Gadgets said as he saluted. "The CIA parachuted this man in two days ago. My sergeant and I were sent in after him. I'm under orders to return him to HQ immediately for questioning. Request use of helicopter and pilot."

"We'll be sending the chopper back to Georgetown for more troops this afternoon, Captain."

"This afternoon's too late, sir. We must leave immediately."

"What's this about? Who's your commanding officer?"

"I'm not at liberty to answer questions. If you have any doubts, please call the general immediately."

"The general?"

"Yes, sir."

The colonel looked at his watch and frowned. A call now would wake the chief of staff, not a wise move politically.

"Can you wait for an hour?"

"No, sir. But I do have a suggestion."

"Yes?"

"Send an escort to the helicopter. Get the pilot there right now. We'll check out the helicopter and make sure it's fueled and serviced. By the time we're ready to lift off, you should have less trouble getting through."

The colonel smiled for the first time.

"Diplomatically put, Captain. I'll do that."

It was twelve minutes before the pilot arrived, pulling on his jacket as he ran. There was no service crew and the pilot had to drive up the truck and pump the fuel himself.

"He's stalling. The pump's going half speed," Courtney whispered from the side of his mouth.

"Corporal!"

"Yes, sir."

"Open that pump and fill the tank. Then get the machine warming up. If you take all day, you won't have time for a coffee."

The pilot grinned and put the pump up to full speed.

"Won't need a full tank, sir. This baby has a long range."

"We will."

"Not for Georgetown."

Gadgets grinned. "When your commanding officer gets through to headquarters, he's going to be given a change in orders. Take my advice."

When the tanks were full, Schwarz, Blancanales and Courtney stood clear while the pilot started the two PT-6 turboshaft engines on the Bell M-212. The pilot climbed down.

"Would you like a coffee, too, sir?"

"Two more coffees would be welcome."

The pilot hurried off, leaving the two armed sentries to watch the three men standing sixty feet from the helicopter.

As soon as he was two hundred feet away, Gadgets whipped out his knife and slashed the cords on Courtney's wrists. Courtney broke into a run for the Bell.

"Stop him," Gadgets shouted at the guards.

Both guards turned to bring their rifles to bear on the running pilot. Gadgets felled the man closest to him with a fist to the kidney and yanked away the rifle. Politician's fist slammed into the side of the other guard's neck, hitting just below the ear. The guard quietly dropped off into dreamland. Then the two Able Team warriors sprinted after Courtney.

One minute later they were airborne.

Two sentries managed to fire their guns before the chopper was out of sight, skimming over the trees, but the bullets didn't strike the helicopter.

Courtney steered northeast out to sea until the town was hidden behind trees, then he doubled back toward shore. It took little time to find the others on a small beach about two miles east of Morawhanna. The rotors whipped up a sandstorm. Courtney was forced to cut the engines as soon as he landed.

It was a tight fit, but everyone was loaded. The children had to double up in the cramped seats.

"Hang on," Courtney called. "I'm afraid of heights, so we're going to be flying about ten feet above the water."

Politician, who was closest to the pilot, asked, "Why so low?"

Courtney turned his head and grinned. Politician wished he'd watch where he was going.

"Keeps out of the way of radar. Besides, choppers aren't like planes. We'll get our best mileage in the denser air, and we're going to have to save every drop we can."

"That tight?"

Courtney held his hand out flat and rocked it from side to side, the pilot's sign for so-so. "Normally it would be an easy go, but this thing hasn't been serviced for a while and seems to be burning rich. We put extra miles on giving them a false bearing to track."

Two hours later Trinidad was a blue line on the horizon. The redheaded pilot headed straight for the island.

"We'll make it," he told Politician. "We'll be landing on the other side of the island from Port of Spain. So the radar won't pick us up at all."

"How about the American satellite station?"

"Won't matter. They'll just assume we're smugglers."

Courtney settled the Bell 212 just outside Guayaguayare on the southwest corner of the island. Politician dealt with the local authorities while Lyons found a telephone.

"Get here as fast as you can," Grimaldi told Lyons. "Hal Brognola's been burning the satellite hook-ups, and he's out to do the same to our hides."

10

Able Team stood uneasily outside the customs area at Dulles International. They still wore the clothing Quincey had purchased for them in Guyana. It did little to make them look like part of the international jet set.

"We're being watched," Lyons growled.

"In these clothes, what else do you expect?" Politician shot back.

The Sabreliner, with its small conference table, could take only six passengers, pilot and copilot. So Grimaldi and Quincey had flown Able Team to the States, while Quincey, the three women and the children had taken a commercial flight from Port of Spain to Washington's Dulles.

At Quantico Marine Station, the Sabreliner's home field, a bus had picked up Able Team and the pilots. The marine driver had expertly driven them over fifty miles of badly connected roads to reach Dulles, which was only thirty miles north of the Marine base.

"The big guy with the bald head standing near the pillar. He's focused his camera on us twice but hasn't shot yet," Lyons said. "The guy in the brown pinstripe's backup. I haven't spotted the other backup yet."

"Spotted more than I did. What do you want done?" Gadgets asked.

"Box him. Wait to see what he does before asking questions."

Gadgets nodded and then made for the washroom. He went in, spun on his heel and immediately followed someone out again. He sauntered in a slight arc that placed the photographer between himself and Lyons.

Politician pretended to be looking through the glass into the customs section. He wandered along the window, holding his jo-cane by both ends, apparently intent on looking inside. He stopped when he was as close as he could get to the man in the brown suit.

Lao Ti moved away from Lyons and stood with her back to a pillar, watching.

A few seconds later Quincey and his crew whisked through customs. They were all American citizens and didn't carry any luggage. The embassy in Trinidad had furnished temporary passports, so they proceeded without delay.

Once through the barrier, they headed toward Ironman. The photographer, posing as a tourist, started snapping photographs with his 35 mm camera. He continued until a short chop to the kidneys made him drop his hands. If the camera hadn't been on a strap around the man's neck, it would have crashed to the floor.

The man, his face taut with pain, whirled and fell into a defensive crouch. He looked up into the face of a grinning Gadgets Schwarz. The Stony Man warrior hadn't hit him hard enough to damage anything or cause unconsciousness. But he knew the photographer was feeling a lot of pain. He looked at the karate cat stance and was positive he wasn't dealing with a nosy tourist.

The man in the brown suit and another wearing a gray one immediately moved in on Gadgets. The one in gray slipped a hand under his jacket as he came.

Politician whirled when his man moved. He lashed out with his jo, tangling the man's legs and sending him crashing to the floor.

When Quincey was a few feet away, Lyons growled at him, "Keep your crew calm."

Lao sprinted across the hard floor and tackled the man in gray just as his Star PD cleared shoulder leather. The man fell heavily onto his face without losing his weapon. But Lao's hands controlled his gun hand.

"Let go. I'm CIA," Lao's victim muttered.

If he expected identification to win cooperation, he was badly mistaken.

Lao began to shout, "Help! Terrorists!"

People fled, and airport security came on the double.

"Okay, move it. Follow me," Lyons ordered Quincey and his group.

For all anyone could tell, the five adults and nine children were also hurrying to get out of the fire zone.

"What about Politician, Gadgets and Lao?" Karen demanded.

"They can look after themselves. We can't afford to hang around until the press arrives," Lyons snapped. "We don't want anyone to know where the kids are."

At the mention of the safety of the children, Karen snapped her jaw shut and obeyed orders. Soon they had joined Grimaldi and Courtney on the Marine Corps bus, headed for Stony Man. Lyons and Grimaldi never relaxed. It was as if they were still in hostile territory.

At the same time, the three CIA operatives and the three Stony Man warriors were herded into a small room for questioning. The head of airport security was waiting to handle that chore himself. He was a short, balding man in his fifties. His suit was neat and his expression harried.

"Would someone tell me what this is about?" he asked his security staff.

They looked at one another and shrugged. One of them finally volunteered to speak.

"We don't know, Mr. Burns. There was a commotion at Arrivals Six. Then the small lady was struggling with this gentleman in gray for the possession of an automatic. She was shouting for help. And shouting 'terrorists.'"

"Actually, these three men claim to be CIA," another security man offered.

Lao let out a derisive snort.

Burns turned his angry eyes on her. "Who are you?"

"Dr. Lao Ti. I'm a computer scientist with the Department of Justice."

Burns became somewhat calmer. Lao's jeans and plaid shirt meant nothing. Everyone knew computer types didn't know how to dress.

"Why did you shout 'terrorist'? Such a remark is likely to cause panic and injuries."

"So could his gun," Lao replied doggedly.

"I told you I was CIA," the man snarled.

"A lie!" she snapped. "The CIA aren't allowed to operate inside the United States." She knew the CIA ignored those laws, but she had already decided on her story when she'd started to shout.

Burns gave her a withering look and turned to the man in gray, "Identification?"

Reluctantly the three CIA types produced small leather folders and handed them over. Burns seemed impressed.

"What's this all about?" Burns asked the CIA operative in the gray suit.

"Just a small agency rivalry. I'm sorry your airport had to suffer because of this woman's thoughtless shouting."

Gadgets and Politician were too interested in watching Lao to care about what else was happening. When Lao started to improvise, she was completely unpredictable. They were fascinated to see what would happen next.

Burns glared at Lao. Before he could speak, she said, "If you believe that, you'll believe anything. Get the police."

"I beg your pardon?" Burns was caught by surprise.

"Either they're CIA or they're not. Turn them over to the state police. If they're not CIA, you've caught some clever terrorists. If they are CIA, I'm going to want to know why they're waving guns around on American soil. Either way I want to see them charged." Her voice was cold, rational, assured.

Burns frowned, unsure how he should proceed.

"Oh, come off it!" one CIA type exclaimed.

Lao pretended great indignation. "That's right! Take the men's word for it," she told Burns. "You could check with one telephone call. These men say I'm a spy, and you believe them. I want the police."

"I didn't say you were a spy," the CIA agent shouted.

Burns outshouted him. "All of you, shut up!" When he had quiet, he turned to Politician and Gadgets. "What have you two to say for yourselves?"

They glanced at each other. They had to play the cards as Lao had dealt them.

"We're friends of the doctor," Politician said in his smoothest, most diplomatic voice. "We came with her to meet mutual friends who were arriving from Trinidad. Now, we've missed them."

"What do you two do for a living? Don't try to tell me you're computer types. I can see you're packing."

"We have permits," Politician answered in a calm voice. "My partner and I own an industrial security service. You can check on us easily enough."

"False fronts," a CIA operative yelled. "They're with Stony Man."

Politician slowly swung his head to look at the man. The Stony Man warrior stared silently, waiting for the CIA man to realize he'd just blown everything.

"What is this Stony Man you're talking about?" Burns asked.

An embarrassed silence fell on the room. The CIA had blurted the name of their most secret competitor. There would be no excuse for the indiscretion.

"Look, we're not terrorists, and we all have government connections," the CIA agent said. "Let's stop wasting time, just let us go."

Burns obviously agreed. "I'll have my men take you to different exits. I don't want to see any of you again," the head of airport security said in a tired voice.

"You aren't going to call the police?" Lao asked.

"If you insist. Would you rather spend the entire day here until we get to the bottom of this?"

"I certainly would. We can't have these thugs running around pretending to be CIA."

Gadgets held his breath. Was Lao going to force them all to go through police interrogation?

Burns and the CIA men exchanged puzzled glances. What did the small woman want?

Politician suggested the compromise. "Why don't you check with the CIA to confirm the identification and ease Dr. Ti's mind?"

"And if they do confirm it?" Burns asked.

"I'll accept an apology," Lao said hastily. "We have to find the people we were meeting. I really can't waste the entire day on this."

Burns raised an eyebrow at the CIA contingent, who hesitated. They weren't anxious to have this foul-up get back to Langley.

Gadgets added his two cents worth to the delicate situation. "I assure you," he said in solemn tones, "if you take the trouble to check us out, you'll find we're exactly who we say we are."

The man wearing the gray suit nodded to Burns. The security chief said nothing, but left the room to telephone.

A heavy silence hung in the room until Burns returned.

"Beat it," Burns told the CIA agents.

When they were gone, he turned to the three members of Able Team. "Why on my territory?" he asked.

Politician answered. "We were meeting friends and they began to take photographs. We had no idea they were CIA."

Burns didn't know whether to believe them. When the CIA operatives reported in, they'd be in deep shit with their boss, whether they had initiated the affair or not. He sighed and indicated that the three members of Able Team should go as well.

IT WAS DIFFICULT TO STRETCH accommodation at Stony Man to include five extra adults and nine children, but it was managed.

Grimaldi was anxious to keep his old buddy around an extra few days. For some reason Brognola seemed to think it was a good idea.

Quincey wasn't anxious to return the children to their parents until they received more therapy to undo the effects of their latest brush with the Church of the Rising Sons.

Able Team didn't want the children sent to their homes until they could do more to neutralize the Libyan fanatics who now publicly called themselves members of the Church of the Rising Sons.

So accommodations were stretched. The only ones to raise any objections were Lisa Frane and Karen Yates. Frane would have preferred a place where there was more freedom and more to do. She settled for a day's shopping trip to Washington. Karen seemed embarrassed about being under the same roof as Politician. Their affair was over, but she felt awkward in his presence.

Quincey's behavior was the strangest, and at the same time the most understandable. His home in Charlottesville had been destroyed. He had no interest in rebuilding. He resigned as pastor of the church on the grounds that he was a danger to others. Then he checked two MAC-10s out of the Stony Man armory and spent long sessions on the target range.

Karen found him on the range the day after they arrived. He had a MAC-10 in each hand and was placing tight groups of three shots, using first the subgun in his right hand, then the subgun in his left. Karen stood beside him, demanding attention, until he put down the weapons and faced her.

"When are you going to start the children's therapy again?" she asked.

"I'm not. I've arranged for a competent child psychiatrist to take over."

Karen took a moment to get over the shock. "The children need you."

"They couldn't need anyone less. I wasn't able to protect them or rescue them when they needed me. And I'm certainly not capable of dealing with this new trauma in the two weeks left before they go back to their parents or guardians."

"Politician says you probably kept us all alive by staying free when my husband and his Arabs took over."

"Politician has a habit of being kind. He's a good man, and he has strong feelings for you."

"Had strong feelings, but not enough to leave here," she blurted. Then she flushed, angry at herself for talking about her personal problems.

"Pol has many great talents, but they come together best when he's part of a team. Everyone, man or woman, should be allowed to do what they do best."

"That's a pretty speech from someone who has just arranged for another therapist to look after his patients."

"It isn't what I do best."

"But you've left your church!"

He smiled ruefully. "I'm not much of a minister, either. What I do best is psychological first aid. That's what I'm going to do. It makes sense for me."

"What do you mean?"

"There are thousands of prisoners in this world. Prisoners of brainwashing cults, political prisoners of oppressive governments. They need a champion. Someone who can take the risks and apply mental first aid during the first week after they're freed."

"And that someone is you?"

"I think that's the highest possible demand on my talents. When I was alone in the Guyana rain forest, I realized that I was useless to those kids. They needed someone to protect their safety. I'm no Rambo. I let them fall into the very hands that could undo, in a couple of days, all the therapy they'd received in months. If I couldn't remove the kids from that situation, I was useless to them. I'm not going to feel useless ever again."

There was such conviction in his voice that Karen had to pause to rethink her arguments. Before she could say anything, he spoke again.

"I'm late for a meeting."

"What's up?" Karen asked.

Quincey made a face. "Hal Brognola's debriefing Able Team. I've been told to be there. I'd rather not. Brognola's not in a very good mood."

"Go on then."

He stooped down and kissed her forehead.

"Thanks."

THE MEETING TOOK PLACE in the Stony Man war room, probably because it had a coded access door and was one of the few places the children couldn't penetrate.

Brognola glowered from the head of the table. His expression was even grimmer than Quincey had feared.

Lyons and Lao slouched on his left. Pol and Gadgets were on his right. Grimaldi, Courtney and Quincey sat at the other end of the table.

Brognola glared at Courtney and Quincey and said, "This should be a private session. But you two have both been involved in this fiasco and should have your say. At least that's what Able Team thinks. What's said in this room doesn't get mentioned to anyone else. That clear?"

Courtney nodded.

"It's assumed," Quincey said in a quiet voice.

Brognola glared at Quincey again, but knew the preacher was right. He'd fought beside Able Team before, and his trustworthiness had been proven. Brognola took a deep breath and began.

"As you know, I'm the White House liaison for the Department of Justice. Able Team answers directly to me, and I answer directly to the President. This causes some jealousy in those few Justice departments that know Stony Man exists.

"The CIA has wanted control of Stony Man from day one. They've never managed to get it, but we've given them enough ammunition in the past few days to help them succeed."

Brognola threw his cigar down in disgust. "First, you overfly Guyana in an unmarked plane. Hell, who are they going to blame, except the CIA? They blame the CIA if the weather's bad."

"Don't blame us," Gadgets protested. "It's the CIA who messes in other people's politics. You can't do that without causing some resentment."

Brognola ignored Schwarz. "To make matters worse, Jack overflies their main airport in a twin-engine job. Guess who gets blamed again? The Guyanese say they want damages."

Grimaldi laughed. "All I did was look for the 747-SP. I didn't see it."

"It isn't funny," Brognola barked. "And now the authorities in Trinidad have a Guyanese helicopter. How do we explain that?"

"Hell," Ironman rumbled. "How else could we get out of Guyana alive? We had proof they were hiding Libyans who are part of an assassination squad operating in the U.S. Cut the crap and tell us when we're going back to finish off those bastards."

"You're not going back. We're going to be lucky if we manage to keep this operation from being swallowed up. There's no question of going into Guyana once more. You really broke the camel's back when you humiliated those CIA agents at the airport." Brognola turned to Lao. "What made you insist on exposing them?"

"They were trying to monitor our operation. They got their fingers slapped."

"They were being blamed for the operation. An operation I never approved."

"Say it out loud," Quincey said. His voice was level, so deadly it stopped everyone cold. "Say they should have left the women and children there to be abused and eventually killed by the terrorists."

"I won't say anything of the kind. I trust Able Team's judgment. It's good. But this time, it may cost us control of our own operation. The incident at the airport was unnecessary and unjustifiable."

"We didn't know they were CIA until we had them," Pol protested.

"But why the humiliation?"

"I wasn't there," Lyons said. "But I trust Lao's judgment. If she felt it was necessary, it was."

"It wasn't," Brognola insisted. "Furthermore, tomorrow you're all going down to Langley to apologize."

He was met with four stares that would have frozen a volcano.

"I could have justified everything else that happened on the grounds that your actions released American hostages from the hands of their captors. That stunt at the airport makes it look like we're deliberately out to discredit the CIA."

"That's like being accused of trying to make a skunk smell bad," Gadgets objected.

Brognola pointed at Courtney. "You go along to make the party complete. You might as well do the flying. I'd send Jack, but he can't plead ignorance. You can."

Courtney looked as if he were going to blast Brognola, but instead he merely nodded.

"Would you like me to go along and apologize for being alive?" Quincey asked.

"You stay here in sight. You're as unmanageable as the rest of them," Brognola barked.

"If they're going to Langley tomorrow, they can pick up Dannie. She lives in Norfolk," Quincey said. "I was wondering how to get her here."

"Who?"

"Dannie Valosky. She's taking over the children's therapy."

"Who authorized you to bring in someone else, and is it really necessary?" Brognola asked.

"I wouldn't have asked her if I didn't think so."

"We'll have to check her out first."

"No problem. I met her in the army."

Brognola shrugged. "Pick her up. But make that apology convincing. Stony Man depends on that."

He stared at the members of Able Team until he received a reluctant nod from each. Then he strode out of the room.

11

Lisa Frane spent a half hour dodging in and out of department stores, making sure no one was following her.

She had started her day of shopping early, hitching a ride into Washington with one of the night-duty staff. She was promised a ride back at 1800 hours. It was an offer she hoped never to accept.

When she was sure her tail was clean, she rented a car and headed southwest. Three hours later she was in an industrial park on the northern edge of Charlottesville. She drove to a deserted-looking factory and slid an envelope under the locked door.

As she straightened up, she was grabbed from behind and spun around. When she saw her attacker, her eyes opened wide.

"George," she breathed. "I thought you were in Guyana."

George Yates said nothing until he'd opened the door and hustled Lisa Frane inside the deserted building. He picked up the envelope she'd left and led the way into an office area.

"Sit down," he growled as he tore at her envelope.

"Not until I get a kiss," she pouted.

He skimmed the letter and tossed it on the old desk. "So they have a secret base in the Shenandoah Valley and the kids are there?"

She nodded.

He stood and strode around the desk and folded her in his arms. "It's good to see you, baby."

"You should have said that before."

"I'm saying it now."

She kissed him.

"It's good to be back with you again. I wish you'd never sent me to keep an eye on your wife. Why bother?"

"We found out the camp in Guyana was safe to use through you. Now we've found out where we can find those interfering bastards that got us kicked out of there. You've done us a lot of good, baby."

"Kicked out of Guyana?"

"They thought the CIA was onto us. It would have been embarrassing to have been found in Guyana. Damn government was planning to kick us out anyway. They had already hauled our plane to a hangar and had it repainted." Yates grinned. "We're now Royal Dutch flying a special charter. Anyhow, I've got a lot of scores to settle with those creeps. Tell me exactly where I find them."

Frane talked for the better part of an hour. When George wasn't questioning her about the layout of the Stony Man complex, he was asking about the children. Who were they? Where were they from?

"What are you going to do to the kids?" she asked.

"We're going to see they get home okay."

She filled him in on as many details as she could remember.

"Try to telephone in reports," he told her. "Everywhere we've made a hit, we've established a base. We have men and weapons at each base. I'll give you the telephone numbers. There's someone at the other end of those phones twenty-four hours."

He took a scrap of paper and scribbled the names of four cities—Charlottesville, El Paso, Minneapolis and Pine Bluff—and the corresponding phone numbers. He handed it to her, and she stuffed it carelessly into her purse as if she didn't know why she'd need the list.

Yates gave her a long kiss and told her, "Return right away."

"Go back! I've done my share. I want to be with you."

"You've done your share, baby. But they might run or something. If you're not with them, we might lose track of the kids. It'll only be for a day or two. Don't get impatient and spoil it all now."

AT THE LAST MOMENT the CIA telephoned to put the appointment back an hour and a half. Rather than change their schedule drastically, Able Team decided to pick up Dr. Valosky on the way to the CIA headquarters in Langley.

The woman who met them on the helipad had to be over fifty, but her sparkling gray eyes indicated that she had a much younger spirit. She watched as her bags were stowed beneath the seats of the small craft.

Her gray hair had been brushed until it shone. She wore it in a blunt cut at the nape of her neck, with bangs across her forehead. The simple dress she wore matched her sparkling eyes and showed off her good figure. The skirt was full enough so that she had no trouble climbing into the helicopter.

"Call me Dannie," she told the group as she shook hands. "Everyone else does. I rode a few transport choppers in the army," she informed them. "This is the first time I've tried a soap bubble. Seems cozy."

Courtney landed the Hughes 500-D gently on the CIA'S Langley helipad. Valosky watched in fascination as they unloaded their weapons to leave them in the helicopter.

"I'll certainly be okay here," she said, chuckling. "I could hold off an Indian attack single-handed with all these weapons."

WOULD YOU BELIEVE THESE MEN CAN HOLD YOU CAPTIVE IN YOUR OWN HOME?

MAIL THIS STICKER TODAY

WE'LL SEND YOU

4 FREE BOOKS

JUST TO PROVE IT.

See inside for details.

A marine detail loaded Able Team and Courtney into the back of a truck and drove them to the old farm house that had been converted into an office building. Already a fuel truck had moved in to top up the Hughes's tanks.

Gadgets looked at the marines' assault rifles; they were off safety. "I think they remember our last visit," he said

Courtney glanced at the guards' grim faces in the back of the truck. "Should I ask what happened?"

"We used their war games so we could visit someone un invited. It meant dusting the instructors' asses with rubber bullets. I'm not positive we've been forgiven."

Courtney rolled his eyes. "How come you guys never mention these things until it's too late to back out. I hope you've noticed that those rifles aren't even on safety."

"What good is an honor guard if they're not prepared, Politician quipped.

The five of them were scanned by hand-held metal detec tors when they jumped from the truck. Lyons's jaw mus cles bunched, but he put up with it. Able Team had left their handguns in the helicopter, knowing what to expect.

From up close, the three-story office building was just as ugly as ever. The guard captain knocked on a door on the ground floor and led them into a large office. The man at the desk finished what he was doing before looking up. He carefully read a three-page letter and then signed it.

When he did look up, he barked, "I believe you men have something to say?"

Lyons looked around. The marine guards were still there M-16s held in combat readiness. It was obvious that the CIA didn't want to work out any differences; they wanted to ex change humiliation for humiliation.

Politician glanced at the color of Lyons's ears and mur mured, "Steady."

"I'm sorry..." Lyons began.

"Sorry about what?" the small gray-haired man behind the desk snapped.

"Sorry the idiots you sent to spy on us weren't competent," Lyons snapped back.

The silence in the room was broken only by the strenuous breathing of one marine guard who battled to keep from snickering.

"Is that what you came here to say?" the CIA bureaucrat snarled.

"What else? If you're going to violate your directives, you might send someone who doesn't stand in the open and take pictures. You might even put a normal lens on the camera instead of one of your homebuilts. And send backup men capable of doing battle."

It was a long speech for Lyons, and it put the rest of Able Team on edge. Would they be taking on the entire Langley establishment with their bare hands?

"I thought your visit was supposed to do something to smooth the relationship between our two firms," the desk jockey said.

Politician managed to speak before Lyons could. "So did we. You didn't seem to have time for civilities, so my friend got straight to the point."

This time the marine made a choking noise deep in his throat.

"What about the fact that the Company is being blamed for two unauthorized jaunts into Guyanese airspace?"

"A navigating error," Courtney said. "Do you know what an error is?"

The CIA man was on his feet. "Stay here," he ordered. "I'm going to telephone Justice about this."

A beep came from Gadgets. As he clawed at his belt, the marines brought their weapons up. The CIA type and the marines watched curiously as Gadgets produced his communicator and acknowledged the call.

"On our way," he told the communicator.

"Stony Man seems to be under attack," he reported to Lyons.

"Seems to be?"

"Five guards didn't report in from duty."

Lyons looked at the still-nameless CIA official. "Do you know anything about this?"

"Nothing."

Able Team turned and ran from his office. The captain of the guard looked to the gray-haired man for instructions. He waved to indicate they should get Able Team out of there.

Standing in his empty office, the head of the Langley site muttered to himself, "Why the hell don't they send me men like that?"

NO ONE KNEW EXACTLY when the attack on Stony Man began. By the time security was sure something was amiss, Quincey, Karen and Norma Johnson had the children on the Stony Man lawn. They were trying to catch up on the children's school lessons.

To no one's surprise, Aaron "the Bear" Kurtzman was with them in his wheelchair. The broad-shouldered paraplegic with his shock of unruly white hair had been an instant hit with the children. In their presence he seemed to wear a soft smile that the Stony Man staff had rarely witnessed.

The Bear's computer room was strictly off-limits to the children, as was the war room. So whenever he could spare the time, Kurtzman left his inner sanctum to help Quincey and the two women.

There had been an attack on Stony Man before. The base had once been devastated. April Rose had been killed, and Aaron Kurtzman had been shot in the spine and sentenced to a wheelchair for the rest of his life. That had been the cataclysm that had propelled Mack Bolan out from under the wing of the government and shaken Stony Man both physically and spiritually.

Sometime just before dawn, a car driving at high speed missed a curve and plowed down four fence posts on the west perimeter. The sensors went wild, and guards charged to the scene.

The young driver was embarrassed and apologetic. He claimed to have been out too late and hurrying to get home before his parents missed him. He was upset when the guards insisted on telephoning his parents, especially because they came to collect him. They lived just down the road.

No one searched the youth. No one at Stony Man knew that he went home to a strong tongue-lashing and the loss of car privileges for a month. Nor did they know that he carefully counted out five thousand dollars when he was alone in his room. He admitted to himself that the amount was high for such a harmless prank.

Extra security was placed at the torn fence. The sensors for the rest of the area were reactivated. Almost immediately the ground sensors blared a warning. Another rush to the west end of Stony Man revealed a stray dog. It was chased off the property, and a tense watch was maintained.

Dawn turned into midmorning, and nothing more happened. Things were beginning to relax when the system of personnel checks revealed that none of the guards by the torn fence had booked off duty. Chief of security hit the alarm button, and Able Team was informed of the situation.

Brognola had been summoned to Camp David to explain the CIA's complaints. The assignments officer, Yakov Katzenelenbogen, was leading Phoenix Force on an operation.

Able Team responded by returning as fast as possible. But it would take the small Hughes 500-D an hour to cover the hundred and sixty miles back to Stony Man.

The security chief dispatched another eight men to cover the hole in the perimeter. They carried Ingrams and assault shotguns. All pretense of normalcy was gone.

They found a situation that they couldn't explain. The day guards were on duty, covering the hole in the defense until repairs could begin. They had found no night crew and had assumed they had withdrawn by road as the day crew had come across the field. All the buried sensors had been dug up during the night.

"Someone used a metal detector to find those sensors. They must have listened to the guards report in often enough to duplicate the reports. But how in the hell did they get that close?" the security chief demanded.

His assistant had no answers.

The security chief hit the klaxon alarm, warning personnel that intruders had penetrated the grounds. Unbeknownst to the chief, the alarm was a signal for the enemy to begin phase one of its takeover scheme.

Half a mile above Stony Man on Skyline Drive in Shenandoah Park, the back doors of a rented van flew open and a recoilless rifle started launching high-explosive charges into space.

The first shells landed wide of the target. Geysers of dirt and the rumble of HE charges surrounded the Stony Man position.

Quincey and Karen reacted to the first sound of the klaxon by telling the children it was time to follow the leader. Karen took the lead and ran for the main building with the children whooping behind her. Quincey had to convince Johnson not to take time to pick up their books and papers, then they sprinted after the youngsters.

Kurtzman sat quietly, refusing to go with them. A Detonics Scoremaster had suddenly materialized in his right hand. When he was sure the children had all reached the main building safely, he dropped the gun into his lap and headed his wheelchair for the workshop area.

Lisa Frane opened the front security door for Quincey, Karen and the children. Her face was white, and she was trembling, but no one had time to do more than tell her to follow them. The stairwell was just to the right of the entrance. Karen led the children down the stairs.

Quincey whipped around the corner to order security to open the war room to them. The assistant security officer did so with a switch in his office. The children would be safest in the war room bunker.

Quincey then sped upstairs instead of down. From the room he shared with Lyons he reclaimed the two MAC-10s he'd checked out of supply. He strapped a Gadgets-type breakaway clip to each leg and threw on a belt of spare clips. Then he was pounding down the stairs again.

"Did you want to take part in the action, sir?" the security chief asked.

"Not directly. I'm staying in this building. I'm responsible for the children in the basement."

The chief nodded, his relief showing. Quincey hadn't gone through any of the Stony Man defense drills. He'd be in the way outside. He was an important extra soldier inside. It was a relief to see the man was thinking clearly, strategically.

The assistant to the security chief was already at the radio, directing state police to the location of the recoilless rifle.

Perimeter alarms went off on all sides. The debris from the recoilless shells defeated the implanted microphones. The shells marched in from the east, shaking the ground and breaking windows. The small guard force inside the Stony

Man grounds hung to the low places, each with a hand over one ear and a communicator over the other. Everyone was waiting to hear where the enemy would come from next.

The HE shells found the main building, but it had been built to withstand such an assault. The false front was blasted away in three places, exposing armor plating.

Nerves reached the snapping point, but no enemy appeared.

Cars in the parking lot received two direct hits, and an exploding gas tank drenched two more. A pillar of black smoke rose over the wrecked cars.

The security force received two assurances to hang tight and keep their heads down. There was still no announcement that the enemy had been spotted. The waiting was a killer.

GEORGE YATES STOOD at an outlook just north of Stony Man. He examined the scene below through a spotting scope. Now and then he barked out an order to someone at his elbow, who translated it and used a hand radio to pass it on to the other terrorists.

"They're waiting to move in," the man with the radio said.

"Not until I see those four hotshots that got us booted out of Guyana," Yates grated. "Tell them to hold position."

"The police just passed the park gates."

"Tell our men to drop eight more charges on the house and then abandon the rifle and van. Have the car drivers move in now to pick them up."

The messages were relayed.

George, like the rest of his trained assassins, wore casual slacks and a loud sport shirt. Binoculars hung around his neck, and a field guide to local birds stuck out of his pocket.

All those within the park were dressed as tourists. Those driving the cars were dressed as women so that the unusual concentration of men wouldn't be noticed.

George suddenly jerked his spotting scope up on its tripod and panned it across the sky. He followed a helicopter for several minutes.

Then he turned to his communications man. "When that chopper lands, the people in it are the target. Tell them to wipe out the people in the chopper and then use the escape plan I set up."

Yates quickly returned to his car. The aide was still radioing instructions as George drove a rented Buick toward the nearest park exit. Twice he pulled over to let state police roar by with their sirens screaming.

12

The four Able Team warriors, their faces grim, looked down on Stony Man farm with its crater scars. No one spoke; they were too busy straining to see signs of invasion and fighting. They saw only the effects of the high-explosive shells from the recoilless rifle.

Courtney flew the Hughes 500-D toward the helipad.

"Land us on the east field, then get Valosky out of here," Lyons ordered.

"I can help," Courtney said as he veered toward the designated field.

"This time you help most by getting the machine and your hides to a safe zone. I haven't spotted any action down there."

"Then why not use the pad?" Courtney asked.

"Someone's ranged in those shells. Wouldn't pay to land where we're expected. Get the machine away. Fast!"

"I'm glad someone thinks of these things," Valosky remarked, her voice calm.

Courtney dropped the chopper like a rock until it was just above the field, then suddenly slowed. Able Team cleared it in five seconds, scattered and went to earth. The door slammed, and the small helicopter returned to the sky in a steep spiral, difficult to follow in weapon sights.

"He knows his stuff," Politician remarked from where he lay in the field.

Lyons grunted as he wrestled with his communicator. The Colt Python filled his right fist. He used only his left hand on the small radio.

"Able Team on site. East field. Status report," he barked into the communicator.

The security chief's voice came back, cool, crisp, "Command turned over to you, Lyons. Shelling stopped less than a minute ago. No foot troops spotted yet. Orders?"

"Stay at communications. Make decisions unless I override. Did you send men toward my position?"

"Negative."

"Then we're about to engage. We have only handguns. Dispatch two with better arms and clips. Otherwise, pull in and hold main building." Lyons gave the flow of orders in a level, clear voice while 7.62 mm fingers of death probed the soft earth to his left.

Lyons rolled to his right before pausing to return the small radio to its belt case. Politician lay ten feet away, worming his expensive, gray suit as deeply into the soft earth as he could. He held his mini-Uzi ready but hadn't started firing. There was no sign of Gadgets or Lao.

Again a Russian-made subgun started probing for Lyons's position. A lighter weapon barked once and the subgun fell silent.

THE SECURITY CHIEF SENT his assistant into the armory, which opened off the security office, to round up replacement weapons for Able Team. When he turned back to the radio, there was an incoming call.

"I'll take Able Team their weapons," the voice told him.

"Are you sure?" the chief asked, then felt like kicking himself.

"Damn sure. Put them in separate sacks and get them to the workshop, pronto."

"Yes, sir."

The chief passed the word to his assistant, who hurried back into the armory for four sports bags.

AS SOON AS THEY HAD touched ground, Gadgets began worming his way to the south and Lao to the north. They then crawled slightly forward of Ironman's position to form a first line of defense while he used the radio. Politician hung back to cover Lyons's back.

Lao and Schwarz were quickly aware that someone was approaching from the northwest. Whoever was coming their way was good. One or two would have managed the approach unnoticed. The group numbered at least ten. It was apparent they'd surrounded the helipad and were taken by surprise when the chopper landed in the field instead.

Lao was the closest to the group's line of travel. She froze while Gadgets slowly worked his way to the other flank.

Lao gripped her Colt Government Model .380 and wished she'd stayed with the MAC-11. She was so small it was difficult to conceal the MAC-11. Only 6 1/8 inches long and 1⅛ inches thick, the Colt was suited to her small hands. Its accuracy was superb, yielding her 2½ inch groups at twenty-five yards. But suddenly the seven-round magazine seemed woefully inadequate.

She shoved a spare clip into her shirt pocket as she lay waiting. It was probable that she'd be in a hurry to reload.

Just ahead of her, a man in camous had spotted Lyons. The invader was crawling with a PPSh-41 resting over his arms. He stopped and fired a short burst, then paused and crawled forward ten feet before firing another in a slightly different direction. He was so intent on his prey that he moved ahead of the group crawling across the field. He didn't see Lao's motionless form, despite her bright shirt.

When he started to fire the second time, Lao placed a single .380 into the side of his head.

Bullets from a half-dozen automatics and subguns snapped over Lao's position. She dug in and waited, not shooting back until she had something to shoot at. She couldn't hear Gadgets's silenced Beretta 93-R over the din, but she was sure he was busy to her left, picking off the terrorists who exposed themselves.

Above the noise she did hear a high-pitched sound, not unlike the chain saw noise they'd followed in Guyana. The bullets snapped about her. Two slammed into her flak jacket.

Aaron Kurtzman was arriving on his infamous all-terrain cycle, determined to buy a piece of the action. The converted Honda 250-ES was a potent fighting machine. It sported a roll cage—whenever it tipped it would roll until it was once again on its three wheels.

Kurtzman was strapped into the oversize saddle. The front carrier held a metal box with a 7.62 mm ammunition belt. The handlebars supported a stripped-down H&K-21 light machine gun. Kurtzman controlled the elevation with a rotating handle, similar to the throttle. The horn had become an electric firing stud. The Heckler & Koch death deliverer aimed wherever the front wheel was pointed.

"Big Red" came hurtling over a slight rise. The machine gun barrel snapped into position, and the bullets chewed earth twenty yards ahead of the screaming vehicle. Kurtzman's white hair stood up in the wind. His lab coat had been left behind, and he wore a shoulder holster on his left side. Four black sports bags hung inside the roll cage.

Instead of driving directly to Able Team's exposed position, Kurtzman drove in a shallow arc and sprayed the enemy with a sweep of 150-grain judgments. He then swung wide and approached Able Team from the other direction.

The terrorists hadn't counted on a one-man cavalry operation. They had little desire to hang around until the All-

Terrorist Cruncher came back to cut another swath. Four of the killers popped up to fire shots at Kurtzman's back.

One fell back with a splitting headache, caused by three 9 mm problems from Politician's mini-Uzi.

A second jack-in-the-box took one of Gadgets's subsonic recriminations to heart—literally.

The last two completely lost their heads when Lyons's deadly Colt spoke to them.

Kurtzman slowed slightly. As he passed each Able Team position, he pushed a sports bag through the opening and let it fall within a few feet of each team member.

Lyons dived for his bag like a swimmer starting a race. He yanked down the zipper and pulled out his Konzak automatic assault shotgun. The assistant security chief had thoughtfully snapped a clip of Lyons's usual load into place. Six rounds of Double O and Number Two mix were at his immediate disposal. He primed the chamber and leaped to his feet.

Kurtzman tossed off the last batch of weapons and took aim at the retreating killers. But they weren't all running. Two lay in the grass, waiting until the last moment to pop up and catch the Bear in a deadly cross fire.

"Roll!" Lyons bellowed in a voice that easily carried over the scream of the 246-horsepower engine.

Kurtzman was a warrior. He didn't assess the situation; he reacted. He rammed the wheel hard right and goosed the motor. The right wheel hit a furrow, and the machine rolled to the left. It did one loop and overbalanced. It came back on its wheels the second time around.

The Libyan terrorists found their target had suddenly moved sideways. They were left facing an enraged blond warrior and the business end of a mean machine. It belched four times. The killers didn't even have time to figure out what hit them.

Four of the thugs reached a clump of bushes on the edge of the property.

Kurtzman was about to do some wood chopping with the H&K-21 when an emergency call from the main building came over his radio. He veered his machine and headed for the Stony Man farmhouse. Able Team also received the call and were jogging across the field toward the same destination.

When Kurtzman passed them, Politician and Gadgets leaped to the roll frame and clung there as the cycle bumped over the field.

The recoilless rifle had knocked part of the false front off the main building. The ninja-trained terrorists had stolen a bulldozer from somewhere and had pushed some cordwood against the far side of the building. Magnesium grenades had set fire to the rubble on one side and to the cordwood on the other.

Pol and Gadgets leaped from Kurtzman's three-wheeled taxi and fanned the area. They met with no resistance. Lyons and Lao came running up. Kurtzman took over patrol and sentry duties while Able Team considered what to do.

"We can get the fire out before the building burns," Politician decided. "But fires consume a lot of oxygen. If the heat ignites anything in there, the people inside may suffocate."

"No time for fancy ideas," Lyons rumbled as he searched through the Konzak clips in his bag. "We want to catch those bastards before they get away."

He brought out a clip marked with a red *X*.

"Get back," he ordered.

The rest of the team took one glance at the clip he was ramming home and ran for cover.

As he ran, Gadgets radioed the security chief to get everyone away from the front of the building.

Lyons stood so he was sighting along the front of the building. He backed up on that line until he was fifty yards from the blazing wreckage. Then he lined up the assault shotgun and sent out six small HE grenades on full auto. They fell in a row within inches of the front wall.

The blast threw him back five feet. Flaming wreckage fell on him, and he was forced to roll over and over to put out the flames before they worked through his flak jacket.

His ears were ringing too loudly for him to be able to hear anything else. He staggered to his feet and looked at his handiwork.

Stony Man, with its armor plate and reinforced concrete, was still standing. But the debris had been blasted away from the front of the building. The force of the blast had extinguished most of the flames.

Gadgets was back on his communicator, checking on conditions inside. Politician and Lao were running for Building One. It had enough fire hose to reach the fire burning in the woodpile at the back.

Three minutes later the steel security door slid open, and Quincey started passing children to the Able Team commandos, who guided them beyond the fire zone.

"How're your ears?" Lyons asked Gadgets.

"Fine. I had them covered."

"What?"

Gadgets made an okay sign with his thumb and third finger.

"Get Courtney and the chopper in here. We have some Rising Sons to set."

"Where's Dannie?" Quincey asked.

"Ironman told Courtney to keep her clear."

Quincey looked relieved. Then he frowned and said, "We have to get the children out of here before those butchers try to kill them."

Karen came and joined the conversation. Johnson kept the children grouped around her. Frane, white and shaking, sat on the grass. The security force patrolled the grounds, checking for wounded.

Soon the chopper thumped overhead. Able Team, Quincey, Karen and the security chief walked to meet it. The walk allowed them to make plans. Lyons's hearing was returning, but everyone had to talk loudly so that he could follow.

"I don't think the terrorists cared whether they killed the children or not," Politician told Quincey. "They needed to distract us to get away. They did it by setting fire to the building, knowing we'd work to rescue the children before giving chase."

"We need a safer place for them," Pat Quincey shouted. He wanted to be sure Lyons heard him.

"What sort of place?" Lyons asked.

The chopper landed, and Valosky jumped out. Courtney killed the motor and followed.

"Get that thing started again," Lyons ordered. "We've got trash to burn."

The pilot shook his head. "Not until we get some fuel."

Gadgets used the communicator once more. "Coming up," he told the redhaired pilot.

Quincey and Valosky had already moved away from the group and were talking rapidly and earnestly. Lyons strode over to where they were talking.

"Get the children out of here," he told the psychologist and psychiatrist. This place is no longer safe for anyone."

The fuel truck barreled up, and a staff member began to refuel the Hughes. The rest of Able Team and Karen drifted over to join Ironman, Quincey and Valosky.

"Dannie wants to get the children someplace remote, away from other people. We're running out of time. If the three women will stay on to help her, it would certainly make life easier,'' Quincey said.

"Unlike some people, we're committed to this project to the end,'' Karen informed him in an icy voice.

"The children will be happy to have you with them,'' he replied in a carefully controlled voice.

Valosky cocked her head to one side and regarded Karen curiously.

Quincey shouted in Lyons's ear, "In answer to your question, we need someplace both safe and remote.''

"Don't shout,'' Lyons complained. "It hurts.''

Everyone stopped and stared at Carl Lyons. They had never before heard him say that something hurt. He stood there with his hair singed, his skin red and his clothes in tatters.

"What's gotten into everyone?'' he demanded.

"How are you feeling now?'' Pol asked in a normal voice.

"What?''

"How do you feel?'' Louder this time.

"Okay. Don't shout.''

"Sit him down,'' Valosky ordered.

It took some persuading, but Lyons finally sat cross-legged on the grass.

The psychiatrist opened the doctor's bag that she always carried with her. She shone a light in Lyons's eyes, first in one and then in the other, watching how quickly the pupils responded. She took his pulse and watched how shallowly he breathed. She touched his skin in several places.

"Concussion,'' she announced. "It's slight, but it's a wonder he's up and walking about. Get him to bed before he gets any worse.''

Lyons strained to make out what she was saying, his eyes riveted to her lips.

"Like hell,'' he rumbled. "We have business. Isn't that chopper ready yet?''

"If you don't take it easy, your reflexes and coordination will play strange tricks on you," Politician said.

Lyons ignored Pol, turning his attention to Quincey instead. "I don't know how they found the kids, but I know just the place for them now. New Mexico."

"Great idea," Gadgets said.

"Where?"

"We know of a place in the Jornada del Muerto in New Mexico," Pol explained. "It was an air force base thirty years ago, but it's been deserted for years. Has the shells of buildings, which is all you need in the desert, and a good underground reservoir. We haul in water every trip and have a gas pump on it. Runway's still usable. Grimaldi picked us up there when this thing started. No one around for miles in any direction. We have the place set up for camping. All we need to do is fly in extra supplies, a few extra sleeping bags and a dune buggy, in case you have to get to town."

"Sounds ideal," Valosky agreed enthusiastically.

"Where's Grimaldi?" Lyons asked the security chief.

"Flew Brognola to Camp David. I sent a 'Hey, Rube.' They should be back soon.'

"When Jack gets back, have him arrange the flight for our guests. He'll get them onto that deserted strip somehow. Wouldn't trust anyone else."

"I'll do that."

"Ready to fly," Courtney reported.

"You go up front," Lyons told Politician. "While we try to catch sight of their ground transport, let's find out which airport their 747-SP's at."

"I'm coming," Quincey said. It wasn't a request.

"What about the children?" Karen demanded.

"They've got a better therapist now." Quincey turned his back and climbed into the Hughes.

Two minutes later they were airborne; twenty minutes later they still hadn't spotted the terrorists. They saw roadblocks thrown up by the state police, but nothing else of interest.

Politician shouted from the front seat, "There's a couple of 747-SPs around. But no plane from Guyana at any landing strip within three hundred miles."

Lyons pounded his fist on the side of the helicopter as if he wanted to beat it into submission.

"They can't vanish into thin air. We lost six men during the night and another three during the raid. I want those bastards. I want them now."

The Libyan ninjas lived up to their name. They had vanished into thin air.

THINGS DIDN'T GET ANY BETTER the next day at Stony Man. Brognola returned in an unpleasant mood after his visit with the President. Lyons had a headache and prowled everywhere, growling at everyone. The other three members of Able Team were almost as edgy.

Politician showed Karen a stern side that she hadn't seen before. He checked an Ingram MAC-11 out of the Stony Man armory and stood over her while she practiced for three one-hour stretches. He was determined that the children would never again be left totally unprotected.

Courtney seemed to be the only one unaffected. He stayed quiet and out of people's way.

The only relief came when Brognola decided to accompany Dr. Valosky and the children to their new hideout. Everyone knew it was unnecessary for him to make the round trip, but no one was about to mention it. Everyone had a sense of guilt that the children had come under attack. Each had to find his way of making it up to them.

Grimaldi had found them an air force C-9. Dr. Valosky, the three volunteers and the nine children were taken to Bolling Air Force Base. Then Grimaldi, with Hal Brognola glowering at him from the copilot's seat, set off for Albuquerque.

The plan was to have the group shop for necessary supplies in Albuquerque. Grimaldi would ferry them by helicopter to the remote site. He and Brognola would return Saturday morning.

EARLY SATURDAY MORNING the night-duty man in communications roused Lyons. He'd been ordered to watch the police and press teletypes for anything unusual.

Lyons took one look at the information being fed through the Virginia State Police and called Quincey.

"Was one of your kids named Lontil? His family in Richmond?"

"Yeah," was the reply.

"They've been wiped. Get to communications now."

Ironman had wakened Courtney and the rest of Able Team. Then he asked the communications man to telephone Brognola and Grimaldi.

"No use, sir. Mr. Brognola telephoned a few minutes before I called you to say they were on their way back."

Lyons frowned. It was good to know Hal was on his way, but why had he left so early? The man just didn't know how to relax.

"How long will the flight take?" Lyons asked.

"Three hours to Bolling, sir."

"Keep track of them. If we find this superplane, we may be chasing it again."

"Yes, sir."

Quincey arrived, still buttoning his shirt. Lyons gestured at the teletype printout.

"Lord!" the preacher breathed.

Lyons didn't give him a chance to go any farther.

"Where next?"

"Huh?"

"Wake up. If they're turning their attention to the families of the children you were working with, where would they hit next?"

"Washington."

"Arm up."

Courtney came running down the hall just a few lengths ahead of Lao.

"We need to get to Washington, an hour ago," Lyons told him.

"Use the 500-D. I refueled it when we landed. Saves waiting for something faster."

"Warm it up."

Ten minutes later a tense group in battle fatigues lifted off the Stony Man helipad.

13

Balentine Usher lived in a Washington suburb where his home looked like everyone else's and his mortgage ruled his life. He struggled long hours in an effort to break out of lower management into middle management, and lived on a take-home pay that would have been scorned by a unionized blue collar worker. When he wasn't working, he mowed the lawn or watched sports on television.

Usher took pains to explain to anyone who'd listen that he hadn't always fitted the mold so well. He'd had his "radical period." However, explanations usually trailed off at that point. He didn't really want to discuss his donations to a group that had gone around assassinating important Americans.

Usher and his wife, Barbara, had been pulled into the Church of the Rising Sons. At Usher's insistence, Barbara had taken their young son and gone to the Church's training camp in Guyana. Usher was one of the converts who'd stayed behind and sent financial contributions.

Until the morning his wife and son, Balentine Junior, had appeared on the door step. Barbara had told her husband what had happened.

Sensei had run the camp like a training ground for the German SS. The children were trained in the arts of the ninja, and the women were given the option of becoming warriors or rewards to successful killers. Then one day a minister had walked into camp alone. He was tied to a tree as bait for his friends in the forest.

Those three friends had come out of the forest, released the minister and decimated a force of over forty ninja-trained assassins. The children and the women who hadn't fought had been sent home.

Balentine Usher had known since his wife had been sent home that she hadn't been a warrior. It had taken days to overcome his moral outrage, but he had finally convinced himself that he was a very forgiving person. The experiences of the Church of the Rising Sons had slowly faded into the background of their lives.

Unfortunately the same couldn't be said for Balentine Junior. He had acquired a firm idea that might was right and was continually in hot water at school. It had soon reached the point where his teachers had decided to expel him.

Balentine Usher couldn't accept such a disgrace. So when other survivors of the Church of the Rising Sons had contacted him, he was ripe to go along with their plan. The man who'd helped free the children had been working with those who'd had problems readjusting. The Reverend Patrick Quincey had seemed to know what he was doing, and Usher had decided his son would benefit psychologically by returning to Guyana.

Usher had known it would be a good thing for his son to receive special tutoring that would help him make up his school year. Barbara was working again to help pay the mortgage, so she couldn't be a volunteer helper.

The few weeks following their son's return to Guyana were restful and restoring for father and mother. So when the doorbell rang late on Saturday morning, they thought nothing of it. Barbara answered.

Balentine's first indication that something was amiss was the sound of horror in his wife's voice when she gasped, "George! George Yates."

"Surprised to see me? We're coming in."

Balentine Usher knew George Yates, the assistant leader of the Church of the Rising Sons. He could speak like an uneducated hood one minute and then turn around and talk like a college professor the next. Whichever way he spoke, the threats behind the message were plain. It was George who had come to Usher while his wife and child were in Guyana and had demanded an additional $2,000 cash as insurance that nothing would happen to his wife and child. Some insurance!

Yates pushed Barbara back into the living room. A dozen men wearing casual clothes followed them. No one had to tell Balentine that the weapons concealed under their jackets shot real bullets.

"What do you want?" Balentine gasped.

"We're here because you let that asshole minister take your kid. Sensei told you Quincey was an enemy of the church. I want you folks to meet Mustafa al-Mugarieff. He and the boys here are the new Church of the Rising Sons."

The tallest of the men stepped forward, gave a mock bow and added in a correct British accent, "Which is no small accomplishment for true followers of the prophet."

"I'm leaving my Muslim friends here. Treat them right," George finished.

"We're no longer any part of your phony church!" Barbara screamed.

Balentine flinched. Was she trying to get them killed?

Yates strode over and grabbed her by the arm, squeezing until she cried out in pain.

"Speak when spoken to. Do I have to start giving you lessons in manners all over again?"

Barbara wilted under the brutality of the attack and the gleam of delight in Yates's eye. He fondled her arm and then her breast before he left without saying another word.

"You two stay still and quiet and you'll be all right," Mugarieff told them. "Make a nuisance of yourselves and you're dead. We're waiting for someone to call on you. It should be sometime today."

Then he turned away from the couple and began stationing gunmen at all the front windows on both floors of the house. Four more men were sent outside to their cars to wait. Another was ordered to watch the back of the house, but to stay hidden.

When Mugarieff was satisfied that the trap was well set, he turned and snapped his fingers, saying, "Strong coffee for your guests." He pointed at Barbara. "You make it. Your husband will serve."

COURTNEY LANDED in an empty school yard. They were only two blocks from the Washington address Quincey had given them.

"Someone has to stay with the chopper. Probably no action, but if the enemy gets smart and tries to take it, the main action will be here," Lyons said. His hearing had returned fully during the flight, and his voice was back to normal.

Courtney sighed. "I seem to get left out of all the fun. I should stay. You may need me to move the damn thing."

"Good. What weapon do you want?"

"Keep your weapons. You may need them. I've had my own piece with me all along."

Lyons raised an eyebrow. "Show me."

The redhaired pilot reached down below the reference manuals in his briefcase. First, he pulled out a box of twelve-gauge buckshot. Next, he produced a sawed-off Viking SOS. The stock had been cut away, leaving only the handgrip. The top carrying handle and front few inches of barrel and sight had also been cut away. The result was eighteen inches of deadly assault shotgun with pump action.

"We'd better speak to Jack," Gadgets quipped. "We can't have him hanging out with deadly friends like this."

Lyons nodded his approval and led the way out of the helicopter. A few curious youngsters watched from the distance, but most of the neighborhood was still asleep. Able Team and Quincey jogged across the school yard and along the street. They carried their weapons, and their web belts were hung with spare clips and enough supplies for a major battle.

They were still a block away when Lyons called a halt.

"There are too many cars," he said.

The other four glanced around. Only a few cars had gone by. They were puzzled. In the block ahead of them eight or ten cars were parked along the curb, and more were in the driveways. That didn't seem to be too many. Then they realized that there had been almost no cars parked on the road in the previous block. In this new subdivision everyone had his own driveway, and it was much too early for visitors.

"If they drove around only one or two to a car, I can see how easily they got through the police lines yesterday," Quincey mused. "What do you suggest?"

Lyons answered by turning left. He led the group to a house he judged to back onto the Usher property.

"Get us through this place," he ordered Politician.

Politician dug out his seldom-used Justice Department credentials and rang the doorbell. The man who answered was in his fifties, overweight and wearing a tattered bathrobe. He had a newspaper under his arm. Politician gathered that the man had already gotten up, but hadn't dressed yet.

The Stony Man warrior didn't hastily flash his credentials. He placed them in the man's hand as if they were a wad of thousand-dollar bills.

"This is an emergency. We need your help."

The man examined the credentials.

"What can I do?"

"Point out the Usher house. We'd like to approach it from the back."

"Come on in."

Politician was taken to a kitchen window. The man pointed across a patio toward a backyard that cornered onto his.

"That man sitting in the patio chair? Is that Usher?"

"Never saw him before, officer."

"Thank you. May we go through your yard?"

"Certainly."

"One more thing. Could I borrow a cocktail shaker, two glasses and your bathrobe?"

The householder took another look at Politician, thinking that maybe he should have telephoned to check those credentials.

"Watch from this window," Pol said, "You'll see how useful they are."

The man's curiosity got the better of him.

Politician ran some cold water into the cocktail shaker so that moisture would condense on the outside. He pulled the old dressing gown over his fatigues and web belt. Then he left by the front door with two glasses in one hand and the shaker in the other.

"Get ready," Politician told the others, who had waited outside.

He handed Ironman the M-16/M-203 combination to carry. While the other four crept to the edge of the house and crawled along the fence line, Politician walked openly across the lawn, lurching twice on the way.

"You're new here," he called to the man in the Ushers' backyard.

The man was lounging in a patio chair, with a gun resting across his lap. The weapon was covered, but Politician knew it was there.

"I do not drink. Get lost!" the man shouted.

The suburban drunk was undeterred. It took three attempts, but he managed to negotiate the low fence without losing the shaker or glasses.

"Everyone has a drink with Silas T. Brown. What's wrong with you?" Politician asked belligerently.

He walked very erect, with the controlled slowness of a drunk determined not to let his condition show.

The lounger's frown changed to a smile. "If you insist."

"That's better."

Politician lurched in his eagerness to reach his newfound friend. The man waited until he was a foot away, then uncovered his gun and thrust it up so that the barrel was pushing Politician's nose into the air. The weapon was cocked and ready.

"All you had to do was say 'no,'" Politician said in a hurt voice.

"Hey, Silas, you're drunk again."

Both Politician and the seated terrorist jerked their heads around. Lyons had made it to the yard directly behind the Usher house and was leaning on the back fence as if he were at home. However, the combat fatigues and weapon collection gave him away.

The sudden distraction caused the terrorist to lower the subgun. That was the only edge Gadgets needed. He had sneaked straight across the fence to a yard next to the Ushers'. Sighting through a hedge he squeezed the trigger of the silenced Beretta. Three parabellums dotted one side of the terrorist's head and removed the other.

Politician calmly walked back to the corner of the yard and put the dressing gown, shaker and glasses in their own yard before rejoining the rest of the team.

Lyons vaulted the fence, handed Blancanales his weapon, then propped up the dead body, angling the chair so the missing pieces of head didn't show. From the house nothing would look amiss.

Able Team and Quincey reached the back of the Usher house without any sign of alarm. Gadgets tried the door. It was locked.

Gadgets produced a small screwdriver that he used to force the molding from the doorsill. Then he slid in the tip of his survival knife and worked the bolt back. The operation took two tense minutes.

With the door open, the five warriors entered the home. They went through the kitchen and stopped to listen.

"This isn't necessary," a man protested in a whining voice. "Just kill these men when they come and let her go."

"Shut up," a cultured British voice answered. "Just hang on to your wife and pray I don't decide to kill her. It wasn't a good idea to add salt to our coffee."

"It was a mistake. I was nervous," the woman said. She didn't sound convincing.

"They have only one child. The only two hostages are in the living room," Quincey whispered in Lyons's ear.

Lyons peered cautiously around the doorway. Two Libyan thugs held automatics to a man's head, forcing him to hold the woman immobile. The tall leader they'd seen in the Guyanese rain forest had a fire going in the fireplace and was heating a poker in the coals.

Lyons transferred his Konzak assault shotgun to his left hand and drew his Colt. He aimed it around the doorway and fired in outrage.

The Muslim fanatic was straightening up with a red-hot poker. The bullet caught him in the back of the head and threw him into the fire.

Gadgets took a short run and leaped past Ironman, landing five feet beyond the doorway with his Ingram MAC-10 in his hand. A quick figure eight cut down two terrorists standing near the front window.

Lyons second shot took out one of the two terrorists holding Stechins to Usher's head.

Quincey was the second man to dash past Lyons. He ran wide to stay out of the line of fire. He ducked through a doorway in the dining area and found the base of the stairs. He stood there with a MAC-10 in each hand.

Lao Ti went through the doorway on her stomach. Her MAC-11 put a three-round burst through the chest of the other sadist who held his automatic to Usher's head. The Libyan managed to put one hole in the ceiling before presenting his blood-stained credentials to Allah.

Gadgets scrambled across the room and began to go through the pockets of the dead men. Lyons double-checked the main floor, while Lao checked the basement.

Balentine and Barbara Usher stood in the middle of their living room turned battlefield. They clung to each other as Able Team moved around them.

When the shooting had erupted on the first floor, two terrorists had begun cautiously moving downstairs from their posts at the upper windows. Quincey counted to three, then stepped out from behind a door with both Ingrams bucking lead. The two Libyan hit men stopped dead. Then they fell the rest of the way down the stairs.

Quincey took the stairs three at a time, weapons ready.

A terrorist looked around the edge of a door, then jerked his head back. A burst of .45s chewed a piece off the door-frame exactly where his head had been.

Quincey became aware of someone on the stairs behind him. He saw Politician charge up with a grenade in his hand. He heaved the grenade into the front room. Quincey sprayed a batch of lead into another front room doorway to discourage anyone in there from coming out.

From one room came the sound of shattering glass and then the whump of an exploding grenade. A split second later glass shattered in the other front room.

Quincey and Politician continued their charge up the stairs. They were too late. The two terrorists remaining there had jumped through the windows rather than hang around waiting for the grenades to explode. Neither man was seriously hurt by the jump. By the time the two warriors reached the broken windows, the Libyans had picked themselves off the lawn and managed to join their surviving colleagues, who sped away from the scene in four cars.

Quincey leveled an Ingram, then changed his mind. People were already gathering along the street. There was a good chance that a bullet would force a car out of control.

"Move it," Lyons yelled from downstairs.

Politician and Quincey were the last out of the house. The dazed couple remained in their living room.

One member of the crowd that had gathered outside was the neighbor who had let Able Team use his yard.

He stepped in front of Politician and asked, "What happened?"

The Stony Man warrior was anxious to keep up with the others. They had to get airborne in time to locate the fleeing cars. The angrier George Yates became, the more innocent people he would make suffer.

"Wrong house. Run like hell," Blancanales advised. Then he was around the questioner and vanishing down the street.

14

Courtney saw the four runners sprinting for the helicopter and started the engine.

"What happened to Gadgets?" he demanded of Lyons, who was the first to board.

Lyons glanced around in surprise. He jumped clear of the chopper to get good reception and pulled his communicator from his belt.

He clicked it once, then yelled into it, "Gadgets! Where the hell are you?"

By that time the others were there. Their eyes searched the street with alarm. There was no sign of Schwarz.

The communicator clicked three times, followed by Gadgets's laugh. "Thought you'd never miss me."

"Where are you?"

"I borrowed the keys to one of our friends' rented cars. I'm following them right now. Better get upstairs quick. As soon as they figure out I'm not part of the gang, they'll try to lose me."

"On our way. Out."

Everyone scrambled into the helicopter. Politician settled beside the pilot and tuned the radio to their communications frequency.

"Gadgets decided to drive. Upstairs. Hurry," Lyons barked.

As the small Model 500-D beat its way into the air, Politician waited for another message from Gadgets. There were

several bursts of static before Gadgets remembered to cut the scrambler from his circuit in order to be read by the radio in the chopper.

"This is Gadgets. Do you read me?"

"Reading you loud and clear."

"We're on the Beltway going west. I think we're headed for Dulles. I'm hanging back a bit to avoid recognition, but I think I'm making them nervous by not stepping on it."

"Hang in. Let us know where you are so we can come for you if they catch on," Politician answered.

"First, find out where Jack is," Lyons told Blancanales "Have to have a plane ready in case we're calling this wrong Then check the international airport again. If they're headed for Dulles, their plane is there."

Politician first let Gadgets know what was happening "We're going to be off the channel for ten minutes. Where are you now?"

"Just crossed the Potomac. Check back when you're on channel." Gadgets's voice sounded strained.

Politician relayed the information to Lyons.

"Hang over the traffic headed for the airport," Lyons told Courtney. "Try to hold a position above where Gad gets will be if he moves with the traffic flow."

Courtney nodded and told Politician, "Let me talk to traffic control first. I have to let them know who we are and where we're coming from. I'll try to get your info for you."

The redheaded pilot dealt with the control tower, warned them he'd be off frequency for a while, then turned the ra dio over to Politician.

Courtney reported to Lyons, "We're batting zero. The only 747-SP that's hung around is a Dutch special charter It flew in from South America yesterday."

"They must have painted their plane," Lyons decided

Politician looked around and told Lyons, "Grimaldi's burning engines. He's just a couple minutes from landing at

Quantico. That's closer than Bolling, and he has priority landing."

"Don't let him waste time going to the marine station. Have him fly straight to Dulles."

Politician shook his head. "I suggested it. They don't have enough fuel to chase anything. Besides, the old C-9 couldn't keep up to the 747-SP. The marines will have the Sabreliner all warmed up and waiting."

"Let's hope we don't need it. We'll be left behind again if we do. The Sabreliner hasn't got the range," Lyons snapped.

"It has as much range as the C-9, but I'd sure rather be flying that SP job," Courtney said. "You can really go places in it."

"Thought you guys liked them fast and light," Politician remarked.

"Grimaldi prefers them that way. He likes fighter planes. I like them bigger and more comfortable. The 747-SP is a real freedom machine."

Then Politician was back to Gadgets. "Are you still mobile?"

"Still mobile, but tacky. We're almost at Dulles, and they're definitely suspicious. They're probably waiting until we reach the parking lot to box me."

Politician repeated Gadgets's report to Ironman.

"Tell him to turn off into an empty field where we can pick him up," Lyons decided. "We don't want a showdown until we see where they're going. We want them all this time."

Courtney said, "Give me the radio. I'll arrange it with Gadgets and keep the tower informed."

Politician passed the microphone over.

Five minutes later the pilot reported to Lyons, "Gadgets just turned south on the Centerville Road. We'll pick him up. Watch for a dark blue car that's driven off the road."

GADGETS STEERED with his right hand. He held his communicator in his left with the antenna extending out the open car window. He was sure he'd been made six or seven miles back, but the cars ahead didn't seem to care. They no longer slowed down for him to catch up.

He'd turned south on Centerville Road. When another sedan containing two men pulled over behind him, Gadgets got the picture. He hadn't been the last man in the parade. The Libyans had him boxed in, and they knew it. Leaving the car behind Gadgets to take care of him, the others continued toward the airport.

Gadgets didn't like the situation. If the Libyans closed in on him and fought, it would be a problem, but one he could handle. If they hung back and waited, the helicopter would be an easy target when it landed to pick him up.

The area was built up, but there were some open lots. Courtney would expect him to turn off soon. He tried raising the pilot, but there was no response. He was probably checking something else with the air traffic controller.

Schwarz spotted an empty field he could reach if he was willing to try the ditch. It was steeply sloped and would require tricky driving. He tossed his communicator down the front of his shirt and steered the car onto the shoulder.

The car behind him also pulled over.

Gadgets's face was set in a frozen grin as he drove the vehicle down the embankment. If he drove at too shallow an angle, he'd roll the car. He plunged down at an angle thirty degrees from the road, not daring to touch the brakes in case he rolled. The car following him took the slope at a steeper, safer angle.

Gadgets was going perilously fast when the right front wheel bottomed out in the ditch. He yanked the wheel slightly toward the left. The right side of the front bumper gouged dirt and threatened to tear the wheel from Gadgets's hands. Then the shocks bounced, and he was driving along the bottom of the ditch. He floored the accelerator, then turned toward the field.

At its steeper angle, the car behind Gadgets was in less danger of rolling, so it could afford to take the slope at a slower speed. But when it came time to bottom out in the ditch, the bumper hit the bank on the field side and dug in. The car stopped cold.

The driver knew his position was hopeless. He and his passenger got out of the car and scrambled out of the ditch. They knew Gadgets couldn't drive far across the soft field.

Gadgets's car got stuck on the border between ditch and field. He opened his door and rolled out just as autofire tore into the car. He had to keep to all fours to keep the car between himself and his attackers.

The first attacker made it to the other side of Gadgets's car. That was his mistake.

A short burst of .45s from the Ingram passed through the tinfoil body metal and tore a ragged hole in the killer's midsection.

The other terrorist threw himself flat in the field. Gadgets couldn't get a line of fire without exposing his head. The Muslim fanatic lined up his PPSh-41 and waited for the Stony Man fighter to play clay pigeon. He paid no attention to the helicopter beating air above his head.

Suddenly there was a roar of thunder from the sky and the terrorist's waiting game was over. So was his life.

Gadgets recognized the voice of Lyons's Konzak. He got to his feet, weapon ready, but nothing happened. He ran for the helicopter as it set down.

The chopper lifted off the moment he was inside. Gadgets was forced to grab Lyons to keep from falling out.

"We won't need a blender as long as you're around," Gadgets said as he pulled himself into a seat.

Lyons wasn't paying any attention. He was straining to hear Courtney above the engine noise.

"The cars went through the freight entrance," the pilot shouted to Lyons. "They crashed through the barrier and sped up to that Dutch plane that's been cleared for takeoff."

"Cleared for takeoff!" Lyons shouted. "Didn't you tell them to keep it on the ground until we got there?"

"I did. Tower just told me that the CIA told him to let it go. The CIA will meet us when we land."

Lyons gripped his assault shotgun until his knuckles turned white.

"Find out where Grimaldi is," Lyons ordered in a remarkably level voice.

Somehow Courtney managed the complicated task of landing and at the same time eliciting an update of Grimaldi's flight from the tower. When they touched down, he reported to Lyons.

"Jack will be here in fifteen minutes. He's been given priority landing."

Lyons nodded, then jumped out and ran from under the whirling rotors. There was no sign of a waiting delegation from the CIA.

"Find out what this CIA business is about," Lyons ordered Politician as soon as he reached his side. "Get cooperation in tracking the 747-SP. I don't care how you do it. Just be back on the plane when we take off in twelve minutes."

A few curious airport workers stopped what they were doing to stare at Able Team, Courtney and Quincey. Since they had discarded their sports bags, they were all openly carrying weapons and were loaded down with spare ammo and supplies. Only Courtney showed any semblance of normalcy; he carried the sawed-off Viking SOS and a case of shells in his briefcase. Quincey had a MAC-10 strapped to each thigh and a belt of spare clips hanging from his shoulder.

Politician nodded at Quincey, and the two of them took off to check out the CIA story. They hadn't quite reached the control tower when a bright yellow jeep from airport security rolled up beside them. Both security officers leveled Police Specials at the two warriors. Their strained, pale faces told Blancanales and Quincey that the security men were fully aware their revolvers were inadequate against the Stony Man weapons.

Politician had been expecting company and had fished out his ID as he ran. He flipped it open to the closest security officer.

"Federal. Take us to the tower and ask the chief controller to step outside."

The security officers were relieved that they weren't being asked to let armed men into the tower. They didn't think twice before complying to Politician's demand. Three minutes later the Able Team warrior was talking to a nervous supervisor.

"They had the proper identification," the supervisor protested. "The CIA officers said I should let the plane go. To do otherwise would endanger one of their operations."

Politician sighed. "What did these men look like?"

He wasn't expecting much of an answer, but the security man who drove him to the tower surprised him by giving a detailed description.

"We keep a close eye on anyone going near the tower," the security man explained.

Blancanales turned to Quincey. "It's the same three we had the trouble with when we met your flight from Guyana. I doubt this is anything official. They happened to be on airport detail again and saw a chance to make us look bad."

He turned back to the controller. "We're following some desperate killers. We'll forget you let them take off if you make sure we're kept posted on their flight."

The nervous controller looked relieved. "I'll do that."

Politician then turned to the security man. "Would you be kind enough to get us to our plane?"

"Sure. Where is it?"

The air traffic controller told the security man which parking slot the plane had been directed to.

When the black Sabreliner coasted to a stop, Quincey, Courtney and Able Team were waiting. They were not surprised to find that Brognola had stayed with the aircraft. His trip to New Mexico had been successful. Conditions in the fast executive plane were crowded, but everyone found some place to buckle in. By the time they were airborne, Politician had filled Lyons in on the controller's story.

"Those CIA types we caught watching us seem to work out of this airport," Politician finished. "I think they just stumbled on an opportunity to pay us back and did so."

"Politics!" Lyons growled. "We need out from this mess. Most of our energy goes fighting men on the same side."

"Don't complain," Brognola snapped. "I take most of the flak. How certain are you of your target this time?"

"A lot less certain than we were last time," Gadgets grumbled. "If we could have stopped the plane before it made its way to Guyana, we'd have saved ourselves a lot of trouble."

"That's history," Lyons snapped. He turned to Politician. "Think we have enough on it to have it stopped before it heads back to Guyana again?"

"We don't have a thing on it except that it's a 747-SP."

"No more talk until we get an idea where it's going," Lyons decided.

Blancanales went forward to collect the information from Grimaldi and copilot Courtney.

While they were waiting, Quincey asked, "The children okay?"

"They loved the flying," the head Fed answered. "They thought they were having another vacation."

Brognola took another chomp out of his cigar before changing the subject. "What about this Courtney? I've had him checked. He's got a good business of his own, financially solvent and all that. Why's he hanging around?"

"You're the one who had him stay at Stony Man," Lao Ti said.

"Wanted him where we could watch him until I finished checking him out. But why's he still risking his neck?"

"I can answer that," Quincey said in a mild voice.

"How do you know?" Brognola growled.

The ex-minister shrugged. "I asked him, and I believe what he told me."

Brognola's frown turned into a grin. He removed the half-eaten cigar from his mouth and said, "Trust a psychologist to come up with a direct approach. Give."

"First, I'm pretty sure Jack is encouraging him to hang around. I'm not privy to all of your secrets, but I gather Stony Man could use another pilot."

"Yeah," Brognola conceded.

"Second, Courtney, like myself, finds what you people are doing more meaningful than what he's been doing. He wants to be part of your group."

"That mean you want to join us?" Lyons asked Quincey.

Quincey smiled and shook his head. "I've got my own way to do things."

Politician came back and sat at the small conference table. There were six seats at the table; he filled the last one.

"We're not headed south, we're going north. Their flight plan says Winnipeg."

"Winnipeg?" Lyons asked.

Politician nodded.

"What do they want in Canada?" Ironman demanded.

No one had an answer.

15

Lyons scowled and repeatedly hammered the table with his fist. "Winnipeg, why Winnipeg?" he asked. And then he bolted upright, released his seat belt and made his way to the flight deck.

"Check that plane's ETA in Winnipeg," he snapped at Grimaldi.

Jack smiled, but his dark eyes were sympathetic.

"This is the fourth time you've asked me to do that in the last hour. What's going to change?"

"Do it."

Jack nodded to Courtney to take the controls. They weren't using autopilot, but were keeping the Sabreliner's oversize engines at maximum cruise in their attempt to gain time on the 747-SP. The Boeing seemed to be flying at a more economical speed, so the pilots hoped to reach Winnipeg at the same time as their quarry.

Jack checked with Winnipeg control. "We'll be staying under St. Paul control to ask for any alteration in flight plan."

He was busy on the radio for five more minutes before he told Lyons, "Hang on, we're doing a one-eighty."

Lyons clung to the edges of the doorway to the flight deck while the plane banked steeply and turned to head in the opposite direction. When they straightened out, they were in a steep descent. Lyons waited patiently, knowing Grimaldi would explain when he was finished on the radio.

Grimaldi looked around and smiled. "Your instincts work better than radar, Ironman. They reported a computer malfunction and received permission to land at the Holman field. We just turned back. We'll be landing there, too."

"Don't commit us to landing until we're sure they're still on the ground."

"It's already too late. They were cleared for takeoff just as we called in. We have to land anyway. These air traffic controllers aren't being cooperative. Turn Politician loose on them while I refuel."

"How long until we land?"

"We were twenty minutes past the airport when we turned. About thirty minutes."

Lyons was scowling when he went back to strap himself into his chair at the conference table. He reported the reason that the terrorists had changed destination in midflight.

"Clever," Gadgets remarked. "Wasn't Minneapolis their first known hit?"

Lao looked up from her portable computer. "Yes, and the second one was in Pine Bluff, Arkansas. El Paso was the third we know of."

Lyons nodded. "Politician, try to get the tower to cooperate with us. And look at their flight plan. You've got ten minutes."

"Ten minutes to get cooperation from a bunch of surly traffic controllers?"

"We take off as soon as we refuel. With luck, we'll be able to get the 747-SP delayed at its next stop."

"What if it's leaving the country again?" Gadgets asked.

"It might be. But it would more likely have landed at Minneapolis-St. Paul International if it were leaving the country."

The traffic controllers at Holman exerted some muscle by refusing the Sabreliner priority landing. Lyons fumed while they spent an additional eighteen minutes in the stack.

"I want you and Quincey to come with me to the tower," Politician told Lyons. "Keep your mouth buttoned, but keep that magnificent scowl of yours. It looks perfect."

"Why do you want me?" Quincey asked.

"Because you're big. Can you scowl like Ironman?"

Quincey laughed. "No one can scowl like Lyons. I gather we leave our weapons on."

"Leave your weapons very much on. I'll flash our permits for them." Politician turned to Lao. "You and Gadgets patrol the outside of the plane. Keep your weapons in sight."

"We're going to look meaner than a starving wolf pack. What's the idea?" Gadgets asked.

"Ironman said to get cooperation in ten minutes. Normally it would take ten minutes just to get to talk to the chief controller. We're going to have to take some shortcuts."

"What do you want me to do?" Brognola asked.

"Stay out of sight. You look like a nice guy. Besides, if we can't bluff cooperation, you're our backup."

"Nice to know I'm of some use," Hal grumbled.

Politician strode down the steeply sloping aisle and told Grimaldi, "Don't ask. Demand that airport security meet the plane."

"Sounds like fun," Grimaldi answered.

He was talking to the tower as Blancanales made his way back to his seat.

A Ford sedan with a flashing red light pulled up to the plane as Lyons popped the door. The two airport security men in the front seat did a double take when five heavily armed warriors leaped from the plane, barely waiting for the Sabreliner's steps to unfold.

Pol strode to the passenger side and thrust his Justice Department credentials through the window into the security officer's face.

"We're laying charges against your air traffic boys. Thought you'd want to be there to make sure everything's on the up-and-up," Pol barked.

"What's wrong?" the officer asked as he handed back the credentials.

"I'll tell you on the way."

Politician, Lyons and Quincey crowded into the back seat without being invited.

"We're in pursuit of dangerous criminals. They let the plane off the ground and deliberately delayed our landing. We'll start with obstructing justice and then see if we can get a link between someone in your tower and the terrorists."

"Isn't that stretching it? I know these guys, and I don't think this was deliberate."

Politician pretended to give the security officer's words some thought. "The damage is done. Someone's got to pay."

The security man was beginning to get worried. "We watched that 747. A group of men arrived in a truck and met the plane at the freight terminal. They boarded, supposedly to fix the computer, but the plane took off right away."

"How many men?" Lyons demanded.

"About eight. They had two wooden crates. Said they were replacement computers. Wanted to test them in flight. Look, those controllers are pretty high-strung. You three go in there looking like you want to shoot them on the spot and we're apt to have an accident. Let me speak to them."

The Ford pulled up by the control tower.

Politician pulled on his lip before saying, "Don't want to cause trouble. Have the chief come and see us. The main thing we have to do is catch those terrorists before they kill again.''

The security officer was so relieved that he ran into the building. It was six minutes before he emerged with one man in tow. The thin controller took one look at the three large, scowling warriors. He took another look at their weapons.

"Ahhh, I . . . I really couldn't get you down—"

Politician cut him off. "How much did they pay you to delay us?"

"It wasn't like that," the security officer said hastily. "We're very busy and just didn't have the time to give a plane special treatment."

"So now we've got terrorists on the loose." Politician stepped forward until he was barely six inches from the quaking controller. "You going to go and explain to some mother that her son's dead because you were too busy to help the Feds?"

The thin man was shaking. He tried to answer but couldn't.

"You think you could possibly find time to give us priority takeoff? You think you just might manage to keep us informed of the whereabouts of that 747-SP? You think you might be able to persuade air traffic control at their next stop to delay them until we get there?"

The air traffic controller nodded to all requests.

"Then get moving. Tell me their flight plan."

The traffic controller disappeared inside the tower and returned less than five minutes later.

"I got on the radio right away. They stopped at Pine Bluff just long enough to take on more passengers and a couple of crates."

Pol and Lyons exchanged glances at the mention of the location of the terrorist's second hit. The controller kept talking, unaware of the bombshell he'd exploded.

"They had just closed the door when the tower got my message. The captain ignored requests to wait and took off."

"Hell!" Ironman interrupted. "Now they know we're after them."

"They're headed for Springerville, Arizona," the controller finished, determined to make a complete report.

"Make arrangements with Springerville to create delays. We'll go there. Thanks," Politician shouted as he headed for the airport security vehicle.

The Able Team plane took off as soon as the three men were back on board.

"It'll take us just over two hours to reach Springerville," Courtney reported to Brognola, raising his voice so the rest could hear. "Our friends' flight time is two hours. Because we're flying triangular courses, we should arrive about ten minutes after they do. Springerville and the Arizona State Police will make sure they stay on the ground this time."

"They leaving them for us?" Lyons asked.

Courtney grinned. "You bet they're leaving them for us. The way they see it, if we're right they'll let us get our asses shot off. And if we're wrong, they'll let us pay the price."

When the redhaired pilot returned to the cockpit, Lyons growled, "Why Springerville?"

"Why anywhere?" Brognola challenged.

"Picked up men at Minneapolis and Pine Bluff. Made hits both places. Probably weapons in those crates. I expected El Paso to be next."

There was a few minutes silence while everyone chewed over Ironman's deduction.

"What's your guess?" Brognola asked.

Lyons pulled a map over to him and studied it. "It's about three hundred miles from El Paso to Springerville. From what Courtney told us, they didn't take all their men on board at El Paso. El Paso reserves could drive to Springerville. It means a raid. A big one.''

"None of the children came from that area,'' Quincey said.

Lao consulted her portable computer. ''My data base on the Libyans gives no one in that area important enough for Khaddafi to want executed.''

Able Team continued to study maps and discuss possibilities. They were unaware of time passing until Courtney paid them a visit.

"The 747-SP's missing,'' he said.

"Missing?'' Brognola snapped. ''You've got to be kidding!''

"They had just booked out of the Albuquerque control zone to the Springerville tower. Their signal was weak. The tower could hardly read them. Suddenly they lost altitude. Claimed to be losing power in three engines. Said they were just past the Gallinas Mountains and were going down. Then there was no more communication.''

"Give,'' Ironman said. ''What's your idea?''

"There's no way they went down in the Gallinas. I was navigating two flights up there, ours and theirs. They either started booking positions with Albuquerque ahead of their real location or they suddenly pushed the throttles to the limit. I'm sure they were booking ahead of their actual position.''

"Why?'' Ironman snapped.

"The tower at Springerville could hardly read them.''

"So where do you think they are?''

"I don't think. I'm sure. My navigation can't be that faulty. There's only one airport in the area that could conceivably handle a plane of that size.''

"Show me,'' Lyons demanded, swinging the map in front of him so both he and Courtney could see it.

"Here." Courtney stabbed his finger down. "Socorro Municipal Airport. It would be difficult but not impossible to put an SP in there."

Ironman knocked Courtney's finger aside and stared at the map. His face was white and his jaw clenched.

"What's wrong?" Brognola asked.

"They landed within thirty-five miles of where we have the kids stashed," Lyons said in a grim voice.

"A much shorter drive for the El Paso contingent," Gadgets pointed out. "They probably secured the airport ahead of time."

Lyons turned to Courtney. "Get us down there fast. We've got to stop them before they reach the kids."

"Jack's already changed course. We're on a landing approach now."

The redheaded pilot was almost trampled as Able Team dived for the Sabreliner's weapons cabinet and began preparing for war. He hurried forward to help Jack with the landing.

"Going in," Grimaldi shouted from the cockpit ten minutes later.

The passengers, back in their safety harnesses, strained to see the airport, but it was dead ahead.

It should have been an easy landing. The runway was in good shape and cleared. The 747-SP was parked at the northeast end of the main runway. The Sabreliner floated in barely twenty feet above the ground.

"We go for the shortest landing," Grimaldi told Courtney. "We don't want to stop too close to our friends. I've got a feeling they're not going to roll out the red carpet."

"That's an understatement. Look at ten o'clock ground!"

The Stony Man flying ace saw a group standing twenty-five yards to one side of the runway. By the time he recognized the recoilless rifle that they were grouped around, it had flashed.

Grimaldi's hand had already yanked on the stick before he recognized the nature of the danger. His right hand gave both engines a shot of life. The plane hopped, but an explosion rocked the underside.

"Gear up!" Grimaldi snapped.

Courtney's hand had already moved to the control. The quick-cycling landing gear would retract in six seconds.

The plane jumped once again as an explosion lifted and then dropped it.

"Part of the landing gear's gone," Courtney reported in a calm voice. Rest is still coming up."

Grimaldi had a choice to make and no time in which to make it. He could abort the landing and do a crash landing at a properly equipped airport. That would be the safest course, but it would let the killers get away. The other choice was to come in under fire. Grimaldi thrust the throttles forward and banked the plane toward the knot of men around the recoilless rifle.

The gunner had been expecting the plane to veer away. The next HE shell sheared off a foot of port wing. The Sabreliner rocked. Grimaldi fought the skewing tendency of the plane and continued to go straight toward the weapon.

"Landing under fire," Courtney yelled to the cabin.

Gadgets voice came back, "We guessed."

The Sabreliner, while aimed at the recoilless, offered minimum profile to the gunner. It bore down, placing tremendous pressure on the reloading and firing. The next shot went wild. Then the terrorists were running to get out of the path of the dying plane.

A subgun opened up from one side. Grimaldi thrust the throttles back and the nose down. The plane dropped, and the bullets stitched the upper part of the cabin. Most of them ricocheted because of the slope of the cabin roof.

Then another burst of fire hit the starboard engine, cutting fuel lines and causing the gas tanks to erupt in a blazing inferno.

16

The decision to go in after the 747-SP at the Socorro Municipal Airport meant a major battle. Able Team had stripped the Sabreliner's weapons cabinet bare, dispensing weapons and ammunition quickly according to need.

Quincey needed only the anger that sparked in his blue eyes and plenty of extra .45s for his two Ingrams.

When Lyons discovered Brognola had only two speed-loaders for his Colt revolver, the head Fed was given the MAC-11 and spare clips that Lao no longer used. She had her H&K caseless and was still backing it up with a Colt Government Model .380.

Lyons, Politician and Gadgets carried their usual weapons. They had loaded themselves with all the spare ammunition and clips they could find as the plane was making its final landing.

A web belt of extra twelve-gauge shells and a backup Beretta 93-R sat in Gadgets's lap, ready to be handed to Courtney. Lao held a web belt with a 93-R and spare clips, and Politician held an extra M-16 2-A. Both items were waiting for Grimaldi.

Anyone who's ever burned a wasp's nest knows the torch must be held over the opening.

The Sabreliner hit the ground perfectly flat, bounced feebly and skidded over the abandoned recoilless rifle. The main door on the port side opened the moment the black plane stopped moving, and out flew a ferocious crew, their stingers blazing.

The servo motors were dead, so Lyons pushed the steps out with huge kicks. Then both he and Quincey leaped to the ground.

Lyons landed in a combat crouch, his Konzak searching for prey. The assault shotgun held a twenty-round box magazine. Each shell contained fifty Number Two and Double O steel balls.

Quincey ran to the other side of the door and held position there. A .45 Ingram MAC-10 filled each fist. His blue eyes had gone icy cold as they searched for terrorists.

Grimaldi and Courtney came charging from the flight deck. Courtney already had his sawed-off Viking SOS in his right fist and the box of shells in the left, which he quickly dumped down the front of his shirt.

Brognola jumped from the Sabreliner and sprinted fifty feet from the burning plane before throwing himself flat on the open ground, facing the same way as the fiery wreck.

Brognola's sprint brought gunfire from a point ahead of the plane. Lyons stepped out from the side of the fuselage and answered with a three-round burst of flesh-shredders that sent terrorists diving for cover where no cover existed.

Gadgets charged out of the Sabreliner and sprinted to Brognola's position. He threw himself flat, facing the other way, his MAC-10 waiting for a target to show.

When he was armed, Grimaldi threw a salute to the burning Sabreliner. Then the two pilots burst out as one and ran beyond the position held by Brognola and Schwarz. They threw themselves flat to cover the movement of the others.

The asphalt landing strip was bare of defensive positions. It was crossed by a secondary dirt runway. Both strips were surrounded by open fields of sand and dune grass. The only thing they could do was stay low.

By the time the pilots had cleared the burning aircraft, heavy autofire was perforating the side of the fuselage where the gas was burning. Politician and Lao had to crawl out the door and drop to the ground. They then ran away from the plane, followed by Quincey and Lyons. Brognola and Schwarz joined the run for life.

Lyons was the first to reach the pilots' position. He gestured for people to split and end-run their plane from two directions. The two pilots and Politician followed Lyons in a wide sweep around the nose of the burning plane. The others followed Gadgets around the tail of the wreck.

Only when they no longer had the burning plane between themselves and their enemies did the Stony Man warriors discover the extent of their problem.

The terrorists who had destroyed the Sabreliner with the recoilless rifle were only a portion of the small army George Yates had assembled. About thirty men were waiting on the sandy field in a collection of four-wheel-drive vehicles. Another twenty were spreading out to encircle the downed plane, which was burning to one side of the runway, about two-thirds of the way down its length. At the end of the asphalt runway, five more held defensive positions around their own Boeing.

Gadgets's communicator clicked. He dropped to the ground to listen while 7.62 mm Russian telegrams crackled over his head.

Politician's voice said, "Ironman says to take the convoy."

"Acknowledged," Gadgets told the radio. Trust Ironman to pick the toughest target. But Able Team had survived by learning to trust Lyons's battle judgment, and there was no time for any argument.

Politician clipped his communicator back on his belt with his right hand while he plucked five smoke grenades and one sodium incendiary from a bandolier with his left. He grabbed his M-16/M-203 and used the grenade launcher to lay a heavy field of smoke between their position and the main body of attackers, who were charging from the 747-SP's position toward the Stony Man group. Then he slammed the incendiary into the M-203 and led the charge toward the Jeeps and trucks grouped north of the main runway.

Expecting the smaller force to charge through the smoke toward the Boeing, the Libyan kill specialists dropped to earth. This took them beneath the worst of the choking cloud and was all the shelter they had from the hail of bullets they expected to follow.

With the attacking force temporarily gone to earth, the eight justice fighters started their counteroffensive against the convoy of four-wheel-drive vehicles. They charged in a ragged skirmish line, firing just enough bullets to force the surprised terrorists to keep their heads down.

When he was close enough, Politician let the incendiary grenade arc over a truck filled with terrorists. As the burning metal blasted into their bodies, a chorus of screams echoed across the field. Those who could dived off the truck. The driver threw the vehicle into gear and started to move. The rest of the convoy followed. The few killers not yet boarded leaped into the lead truck and stomped out the small blazes in the truck bed.

Most of the convoy had been beyond the truck that led the retreat. In all, six vehicles of terrorists got away. With the major part of the enemy force speeding away from the scene, Able Team turned their attention to the more than twenty killers who remained. They had discovered that Able Team wasn't charging them, so they were emerging from the smoke, determined not to let the eight warriors get away.

The Stony Man fighters took cover in a slight depression in the ground. It was barely enough to hide them from enemy fire, provided that the enemy didn't get too close. The eight lay in a semicircle, facing the charging Libyans.

Politician used the M-203 to send a wire-wound grenade into the midst of one charging group. Two men went down. Two more were wounded. Those who survived spread out.

Lyons's Konzak bellowed defiance and destruction. More of the charging fanatics were smashed to earth. Those who weren't suddenly desired lower profiles and dived for the grass.

Lao used her caseless to snipe at the standing targets farther away. She downed two before the rest of the killers decided to hit the ground. The war evolved into a deadly game of tag in which all the contestants crawled around on their stomachs.

Quincey fired one clip in a slow arc, allowing the bullets to clip grass as they flew. He was rewarded with a scream of terror.

He slapped a fresh clip into the Ingram and muttered, "Not efficient enough."

Ironman spoke to the entire group, pitching his voice just loud enough to be heard above the roar of the burning plane. "We need their plane and we need it in flying shape. Any suggestions?"

"Keep them busy until Lao and I get in position to protect the plane," Gadgets said.

Lyons grunted and nodded.

Schwarz and Lao rolled to their feet and sprinted away from the Boeing and the encircling enemy, retreating through the heat and smoke from the blazing Sabreliner. The other six laid down a heavy covering fire. Bullets snapped the air around Lao and Gadgets, but their zigzag running kept them safe.

Once out of range of the enemy subguns, Lao and Gadgets settled down to a distance-eating run. They were used to the pace; Ironman had them run it for five miles every morning that they weren't in action. They slowly arced away, circling the landing field out of range of enemy fire.

Somewhere in the distance sirens screamed. Someone in one of the few houses west of the landing field must have considered the shooting worthy of a call to the state police.

Gadgets and Lao continued toward the Libyans' plane. They were spotted by the terrorists, and a group of six was sent to intercept them. The two Stony Man warriors paid little attention to the approaching squad.

"Now," Lao snapped.

Gadgets stopped and bent forward, bracing his hands on his knees. Lao stood behind him and steadied her G-11 caseless across his shoulder. The terrorists were still two hundred yards away, but closing fast. When they saw what Lao was doing, they brought up their subguns and opened fire.

"Now," Lao said calmly.

Gadgets expelled some air from his lungs, then held his breath. Lao held her breath, too. Then, using Gadgets as a bench rest, she returned the enemy fire with a series of long bursts.

Two hundred yards was too great a distance for the PPSh-41 and its light pistol ammunition. The distance was manageable for the caseless.

One terrorist tried throwing himself flat, but was still a good target for Lao from her standing position. Five seconds later, only one terrorist was breathing and he showed a sudden desire to rejoin his comrades. He managed to run three paces before Lao's firing brought him down.

Lao and Gadgets expelled their breaths and gasped for air. It was impossible to control their breathing after a hard run, and only by holding their breaths were they steady enough for Lao to score from two hundred yards.

They ran up to the bodies and went to earth. A slight roll in the land barely concealed them from the area where the other six lay, surrounded. While Lao watched for more terrorists, Gadgets pulled on combat fatigues taken from a dead terrorist his size. He gathered up his web belt and MAC-10 in its leg clip, added Lao's G-11 and rolled them in his own fatigues.

He picked up a PPSh-41 and searched the bodies until he could ram home a fresh clip. He then tucked his bundle under his left arm and marched toward the 747, aiming the Russian-made subgun at Lao. She fumbled with her small Colt .380 for a moment, then walked ahead of him with her hands clasped on the back of her neck.

The firing was heavy around the depression where the other six were now completely encircled by Libyan killmasters. Gadgets felt the need to rush, but knew it wouldn't look right if he ran his prisoner.

The terrorists weren't getting everything their way. They had to keep moving around the trapped warriors. Whenever Politician noticed firing coming from a fixed location, a grenade would arc out from the depression to explode over the hapless gunner who'd fired too often from one location.

It was a telling technique, but Gadgets knew Politician would run out of grenades before he ran out of targets to use them on.

The plane sat a quarter mile from the fighting, with an extension ladder reaching up to her passenger door. One of the five guards between the fighting and the plane looked around at Gadgets. Schwarz kept his face partially turned away and hoped the different camous would let him get away with the masquerade. It must have worked. The guard returned his attention to the battle zone.

It was a difficult climb up the ladder. Gadgets was forced to keep the subgun in one hand and had the bundle in the other. He solved his problem by putting the sling of the PPSh-41 around the bundle and tucking it under his gun arm. He climbed with his left hand while the right struggled with both weapon and bundle.

He finally managed to step into the dimness of the plane only to find that both he and Lao were covered by a man waving a Stechin automatic.

"Welcome," the man said with a midwestern twang. "Considerate of you to pay us a visit. Drop your gun."

Two other men in pilot uniforms stayed in the background. They didn't seem to be armed.

Gadgets stepped to one side and swung the subgun toward the armed pilot. The Stechin was moved to target acquisition, centering on Gadgets's face.

Lao had been waiting for that move. Her right arm straightened with a snap. The small automatic slid out of the loose sleeve of her fatigues and into her hand. Before the pilot realized he'd been suckered, a .380 ACP had scrambled his brains.

The other two members of the flight crew raised their hands and submitted to the quick application of plastic cuffs.

Lao set off to check the plane for more occupants. Gadgets extended the aerial on his communicator and held it out the door.

"Plane under control," he announced.

Politician's worried voice came back, "We can't get our heads up far enough to see the damn plane."

"Hold on for five more. The marines are coming."

Gadgets put on his own fatigues while he waited for Lao to finish checking out the plane. He was much more worried about being shot by his comrades than by being recognized by the enemy.

When Lao gave the all-clear sign, he said, "Hold the plane. I'm rounding up passengers."

"Don't forget the flight crew."

He grinned at her as he buckled on his web belt and MAC-10. Then he grabbed the ladder and scrambled down. The sound of sirens was close. There was a problem that the police might stumble into the middle of a war they weren't equipped to fight.

The five killers guarding the 747-SP swung to face him, muttering oaths as they brought their weapons up.

Tight bursts of 4.77 mm slugs from Lao's caseless spun two of them into the hands of death.

Gadgets leaped from the ladder, snatching his MAC-10 from its clip as he jumped. He landed and tucked and rolled to one side. Then he came up shooting. A figure eight of .45 slugs knocked two terrorist guards right into the next world.

The last guard was diving and rolling to escape the two lines of fire. One from Gadgets, and the other from the open forward door of the plane. Gadgets waited calmly until the terrorist stopped moving. When the Libyan looked up to see why the firing had stopped, a three-round burst grouped tightly around his left eye.

Gadgets knew it was all or nothing. He jogged toward the battle zone. When he spotted enemy in the grass, he stopped, lined up carefully and nailed them where they lay. A couple of bullets cracked close to him from the far side of the encirclement, but the gunner paid for his shots. A boom from the Konzak removed the top of his head.

Then Gadgets ran around the outside of the terrorists' circle, sending .45 caliber greetings to each one he saw. The Libyans all brought their weapons to bear on the new menace—a definite mistake.

Six fighting maniacs exploded from the depression where they'd been pinned.

Courtney fired his sawed-off twelve gauge as fast as he could pump it. His rapid fire cleared the way for Politician and Grimaldi to start working the circle with their M-16s. Brognola and Quincey both popped up with Ingrams blaz-

ing, sweeping their quadrant with enough lead to sink four
terrorists.

Lyons rolled out of the depression with the assault
shotgun on full-auto. He raked a wide area with steel pellets, eliminating another three killers.

Seven seconds after Gadgets had begun working the outside of the circle, the Stony Man force ran out of targets.
Two patrol cars screeched along the runway toward their
position.

"Politician, get them off our backs. We're running out of
time," Lyons snapped.

Everyone knew Ironman was upset. He was telling them
something they already knew. They were all thinking of the
children and of the ten-minute head start enjoyed by a convoy of insane terrorists.

17

Politician sprinted in an arc that took him past Hal Brognola. The head Fed was feeding another clip into the Ingram MAC-11 when Politician motioned for him to help intercept the two state police cruisers that sped onto the runway.

Lyons dispatched Gadgets and Quincey to see what had happened to the airport staff, then he waved Grimaldi and Courtney over to him.

"Good fighting. Now I need good flying. Can you get that monster into our camp where the kids are?"

"Not likely," Grimaldi answered.

"Runway too short?" Courtney asked.

"Not theoretically," the Stony Man pilot answered, "but I chewed up a lot of the runway landing the Sabreliner, because of sand cover. It added half a mile to my stopping distance."

"We'll never catch up to those killers if you don't," Lyons said. "They've got too much head start. They'll take to the desert where the state troopers can't follow. A helicopter would have to come from Albuquerque. We don't have time for that."

"Let's not stand here guessing," Courtney said. "Let's see if the bird is fit to fly before we waste more time speculating."

Lyons didn't answer. He started running toward the ladder propped against the 747-SP, Courtney at his heels. After a split second's hesitation, Grimaldi followed.

Lyons stepped into the 747-SP and saw Lao covering the two prisoners.

"Who are they?" he demanded.

"Crew. American. They weren't armed. Surrendered when we shot the one crew member who was."

"We're just hired pilots," one protested. "We didn't even know they were doing anything illegal until today."

Lyons looked at them speculatively. His cold eyes silenced the pilot who had spoken.

"Have them follow us to the flight deck," Lyons told Lao. "Our guys may have some questions for them."

They climbed the spiral staircase two levels. Lyons, Grimaldi and Courtney stepped onto the flight deck. Lao held the two captives at gunpoint outside the open door.

Courtney slid into the pilot's chair. "Jack, start a systems check."

Ironman raised an eyebrow at the Stony Man pilot.

Grimaldi slid into the engineer's seat toward the rear of flight deck and began flipping switches.

As he worked, he explained to Lyons, "If this baby takes off, Courtney will be in the pilot's seat. I can fly rings around him in anything with one or two engines—"

"Cannot," Courtney interrupted.

Grimaldi's grin stretched a little wider, but he made no response to the redheaded pilot. Instead he finished his explanation. "But in these big jobs, the guy has about a hundred times the flying hours I have. I don't think we can land this at your hideout, but I'll let him make the call."

"You're nuts if you try," a voice said from the doorway.

Grimaldi and Lyons glanced at the man who had spoken. The hair at his temples held just the right trace of gray, and his flight uniform was spotless. His brown eyes held Grimaldi's darker brown.

"Flight chart by the copilot's chair. Look for yourself. You're going to have a steady crosswind of thirty knots. Add that to an ancient runway covered with sand. The total comes out suicide. The guy the little lady shot was the only crewman who belonged to the gang. They wanted us to go in there. We refused because it's suicide. Not even guns pointed at us could change my mind."

"You refused the captain?" Lyons prompted.

The prisoner let out a snort of contempt. "He was captain because he was one of them. He knew enough to push buttons. Did everything on auto, landing, taking off, the works. If there was any real flying needed, he turned the plane over to Chuck and myself. When we refused, it was a cinch he wasn't going to try it. So he convinced the others that the landing was impossible. For once he was right."

"What condition is this crate in?" Courtney asked.

"Pretty good, actually. It's almost new. Maintenance has been kept up, believe it or not."

"He's right about the crosswinds," Grimaldi said, looking up from the weather report he was studying.

Courtney glanced up from his check. "How're the systems?"

"All go," Grimaldi admitted.

Courtney plucked the charts out of Grimaldi's hand. He gave the weather chart a cursory glance, then leafed through the rest. "Tell me about the landing field."

"Seven thousand feet, northeast to southwest, two hundred wide, a few buckles that were never fixed. Wind seems to keep it pretty clear, but there's always drifted sand over parts of it," Grimaldi rattled off.

"The wind's from the west at the moment, but I think we can do it."

Grimaldi didn't look at his friend. Instead he looked at the two members of the terrorists' flight crew.

"We need a second officer," he told them.

"Not me," the talkative one said. "You go in on this and you leave me behind."

Lyons butted in again. "You don't understand, friend. You're both accessories to murder one. You're both coming. The only question is whether it's on the flight deck or in the cargo hold."

"You can't do that."

"Did you tell your friends that when they went out to murder?"

"We didn't know anything was wrong with the setup until today. No reason to kill us."

The silent one finally spoke. "If I help, do you put in a good word for me?"

Lyons nodded.

"You got a second officer."

"Fool," the talkative one said.

Grimaldi looked up at Lyons and said, "If Courtney says it's worth a try, it's worth a try."

"Don't just sit there then. I'll go and get the others. Lao, come and help me with this one."

Lyons left the flight deck, pushing the talkative pilot ahead of him. Lao followed, puzzled. Lyons certainly didn't need her help to handle him.

Lyons paused at the open door and saw that the others were making their way toward the plane.

Then he shoved the pilot into the first-class lounge and into a seat. Once the man's seat belt was in place, Lyons attached each wrist to the seat frame with plastic cuffs. By the time he was through, the first engine was firing up.

He drew Lao out of earshot and told her, "You're suddenly struck with the romance of flying. I want you to hang around the flight deck with stars in your eyes. Keep a close watch on our volunteer.''

''Why? I don't know anything about flying.''

''You're an engineer and scientist. He can't snow you, but you can snow him with your ignorance.''

She grinned. ''I'll do my best.''

Politician was the last one up the ladder. He and Quincey stowed it, then they made their way to the passenger area. Politician went straight to Lyons to report.

''Hal and I managed to straighten things out in a hurry, but I don't think we'll win any popularity contests in this state. They'll have one of their helicopters overfly the camp just in case.''

''The airport people were okay,'' Gadgets added. ''You were right about terrorists driving up from El Paso. They locked the staff in a storage room and took over until the 747-SP came in. We were right behind them, so all the terrorists were too busy to worry about the staff again. They seem to be on the up-and-up.

''Good.'' Lyons used the one word to cover both reports then he sat down and buckled in across the aisle from the prisoner.

''You're really going through with this?'' the prisoner asked.

Lyons nodded.

''You realize this buggy will break up into a million pieces on landing.''

Lyons turned his blue eyes to the prisoner. ''If those goons you've been ferrying around kill the children they're after, how soon will you forgive yourself?''

''Why should they go after mere kids?''

''It's the way terrorists work. If the crimes are senseless enough and outrageous enough, people back off with terror. Most people don't know how to deal with insane killing.''

"I suppose you do."

Lyons raised his assault shotgun and patted it. The pilot looked away as the plane taxied to the end of the runway. When it started to turn once more, making a 180-degree turn so it could take off into the wind, the pilot spoke rapidly.

"We're going to make the turn on a runway a hundred and fifty feet wide," the ex-first officer of the craft mused. "That pilot of yours must be pulling the handle right off the tiller. I suppose it's too late to volunteer for flight duty?"

"It is."

"I'm better than Jessop. I never quite trusted that man."

"Must have made for a great group in the cockpit. No one trusted anyone else."

The pilot was silent before saying, "Guess that describes it. It's strange. It's very close on a flight deck. You usually get to know the other guys in the crew. You respect them, or you ship out. That would never have developed with this crew."

The plane started to blast down the runway.

"Hope those guys know what they're doing. This is a hell of a tricky takeoff. High altitude here means the air isn't as dense. A lot less lift. We're headed straight at some power lines. After that, the mountains are less than a mile and a half away. I'm losing the feeling in my hands. Please undo the cuffs."

Lyons stared at him for a moment, then produced a knife that went through the cuffs as if they were made of string.

"Leave the belt done up until I tell you to undo it."

"You got it."

The plane left the runway, climbed for a few seconds, then went into a hard forty-five degree bank turn until it was facing east. Then once more it began a slow climb.

"Couldn't get away with a turn like that if you had paying passengers," the pilot breathed. "But it's the best way to make a short trip in an awful hurry. These guys might just know what they're doing. But that runway's impossible. No way of holding a sandy runway in a crosswind."

Lyons shrugged, leaned back and closed his eyes.

LAO SLIPPED UP to the flight deck just before takeoff.

"I want to see you work," she told Grimaldi.

"Who? Me? I'm here only for the flying lessons. I'm going to learn how to give a copilot a heart attack before you're ten feet off the ground."

"What's that mean?" she asked. But her eyes were studying the systems board in front of the flight engineer's seat.

"We don't have time to climb the mountains," Courtney explained. "Even with all our circling we're only going about a hundred miles. If we went straight ahead, we'd have to go up to eight thousand and then back down. That would take too long. Besides, I can't stand heights."

"He's insane," the stranger in the flight engineer's seat said as he opened a panel and busied himself with the switches inside.

Lao caught his hand in a grip like a bench vise. She leaned forward and squinted at the switch labels. The flight engineer balled his left fist, but forgot to use it when she increased the pressure on his right hand. Instead, he yowled with pain.

"Jack," Lao asked in a level voice, "should this guy be switching generator switches to an off position?"

"What!" Grimaldi was out of his seat in a flash. He took one look at the board and slammed a right cross that knocked the flight engineer unconscious.

Jack's hands danced across the board while Lao pulled the man out of his seat.

"Everything's okay now," Jack explained. "But he took three generators off-line. The other was bound to blow from the overload. We wouldn't have had much space to rectify things at this altitude. Take over, Lao."

Courtney's only comment was, "Flap five degrees," as soon as Grimaldi was back in the copilot's chair.

Grimaldi hit the servos that extended the width of the wing, bringing the extensions in until they formed only a narrow extension of the wings.

Lao dragged the unconscious man out of the flight deck. She stepped over him to the top of the spiral staircase and yelled for another member of Able Team to come and get him. By the time she was buckled into the engineer's seat, the plane was nosing down toward the desert.

Jack told Courtney, "East another ten degrees or we'll miss it. Do you want the gear down?"

"Uh-huh. We'll take this baby in on its wheels."

"We'll tear them off if we lose the runway."

"That it ahead?"

"Yeah. You'll have to redo the approach. The wind's taking us in too far off to correct."

Courtney kept on course. "Don't intend to go down this time, but I want to be low and slow. Can't land this bird on your memory."

"Look to your right," Lao snapped.

Grimaldi looked. Courtney concentrated on the runway.

"The Libyans are about five miles away," Grimaldi reported in a calm voice.

"It'll be touch and go," Courtney admitted as he pulled the plane up and around, feeding it more fuel.

"I'll go warn everybody," Lao said.

"Use the intercom," Jack said. "Everyone stays buckled until this thing stops."

"Wheels down. Full flap," Courtney ordered. Sweat was beginning to collect in his sideburns.

Jack Grimaldi hit the necessary switches immediately. "You think we'll keep our wheels?" he asked the pilot.

"Damned if I know. Those crosswinds have put a couple of sand drifts a foot deep on that runway. We may leave the wheels behind, but that's better than dipping wings into that sand."

"Aren't you glad we don't own this baby?" Jack quipped. "The salvage bill is going to be fierce."

"I'd pay it. She flies like a dream."

Lao figured out the intercom. "Stay buckled until we come to a complete stop. Then go like hell. We'll be arriving less than a minute before the convoy that left us in Socorro."

Courtney and Grimaldi were paying no attention to Lao. They were both completely focused on getting the plane up and around for a second pass at the runway. The plane was making a banked turn that threatened to dip a wing in the sand. Then they straightened and climbed for two minutes before going into another sharp turn.

"Don't tell me. Let me guess," Lao said in a dry voice. "You both always wanted to be crop dusters."

"Told you I was afraid of heights when I first flew you out of Guyana," Courtney answered.

Then the big bird was heading toward the almost invisible runway. The plane had to face partly into the wind in order not to be blown off course. So the tip of the port wing led the tip of the starboard wing by about fifteen feet. The sensation of moving sideways was exaggerated until it felt as if Courtney were bringing the plane in at a forty-five-degree angle.

The plane settled rapidly, and the rolling sand flashed by in a blur. At first Lao thought they were going to land short of the runway. Then the ribbon of black seemed to drift away with the wind, and the 747-SP came down toward the sand on the upwind side. The rising waves of sand were so close that Lao listened for the thump of the first one hitting the plane, but she didn't hear it.

Courtney increased the thrust to the starboard engines. The plane straightened with respect to the runway and was blown back into line with it. They settled onto the runway smoothly, but then the nightmare began. The plane shuddered and leaped as if a big hand were slowing it, then letting it go only to drag it back. The waves of sand were slowing the plane.

The reverse thrusters were already sticking up, and Courtney had the port and starboard throttles in separate hands. The engines were roaring as they did just before takeoff. Grimaldi worked feverishly with the foot brakes attached to the wheels, but the antiskid computer was negating most of his effort.

The plane skidded down the runway like a drunken sailor, fighting Courtney's control every foot of the way.

Suddenly one rocking wing caught the tip of a wave of sand and the plane began to spin. Courtney's hands flew like lightning, keeping up reverse thrust on one side and cutting the reverse on the other.

"Even braking," he demanded of Grimaldi.

Jack was puzzled, but complied immediately.

Then Courtney cut the reverse thrust on the second side and they charged down the sand-covered runway, the tail slowly taking the lead.

When they were going almost backward, Courtney killed the spin with a small thrust on the starboard engines. Then he started feeding gas more evenly to the jets. This time they shoved the plane forward against its own momentum. He still controlled the left and right engines with separate hands, fighting the plane's tendency to spin out from his control.

With the engines thrusting against their momentum, they stopped quickly. Then both pilots moved to shut down systems before there was a fire. When they were through, Jack reached over and squeezed his friend's shaking shoulder.

"Best damn landing I ever witnessed," Jack said.

Lao released her harness and ran for the exit to get her H&K caseless that was still in the passenger area. She negotiated the spiral staircase slowly. The plane had come to rest with one wing almost touching the sand. The slant made the staircase very awkward to use. She reached the next level in time to see Politician and Gadgets finish lowering the extension ladder to the ground.

The only people left in the passenger section were the two prisoners.

"What do we do?" asked the one who wasn't wearing plastic cuffs.

Lao didn't have time for complex discussions. She snatched a pair of cuffs from her belt and handcuffed the prisoner to the arm of a seat.

"Relax and wait," she told him.

She grabbed her assault rifle and was gone.

THE LANDING GEAR HAD BEEN heavily damaged in the landing. The 747-SP leaned over at a fifteen-degree angle, and one wing rested on a wave of sand. Fortunately the door was on the low side of the plane.

Ironman hadn't waited for the ladder. As soon as the door was open, he jumped out backward, catching the doorsill in his hands. He hung for a second and then dropped the remaining eight feet. He kept his footing by landing in a deep squat. Then he straightened and ran toward the cluster of tents two hundred yards west of the plane.

One solitary figure had emerged and was heading toward the 747-SP. The small figure wore fatigues and a wide-brimmed straw hat. Lyons couldn't identify the person until she stopped and spoke.

"You!" Karen sounded shocked.

Lyons stopped and looked around, making an instant assessment of the tactical and strategic considerations. The

747-SP had stopped just where the runway curved into an apron area. The shells of old hangars remained in that area, but their corrugated metal walls would be no protection from terrorist bullets.

Beyond the tents to the west, Lyons saw plumes of sand, indicating that the terrorists had intentionally swung wide when they saw the plane land. They now approached the camp, keeping the tents between themselves and the Stony Man force. They obviously knew that Able Team had taken over the plane.

Lyons pointed toward the approaching force. "Your husband and colleagues. Get everybody into the biggest building. Have them lie flat on the floor."

"Can't you get us out of here?"

"Look at the landing gear, woman. We're not going anywhere. The walls won't stop bullets, but at least they won't be able to see their targets. Move your ass!"

With that thunderous command ringing in her ears, Karen turned and ran. She dashed for the large canvas fly where everyone was having an afternoon siesta until the heat of the day passed. She ran all out, but Ironman was way ahead of her, dashing to place himself between the children and the approaching terrorist force.

Then Quincey, Politician, Gadgets, Brognola and the two pilots also passed her, all running to cover the retreat of the children to a safer place.

"We have to move to the old hangar," Karen yelled as soon as she reached the group under the fly.

Dr. Valosky was on her feet immediately, organizing an orderly evacuation.

Leaving Dannie, Norma and Lisa to get the children moving, Karen ran for her tent. Suddenly she was thankful that Politician had given the MAC-11 to her.

It was missing from her suitcase!

Karen was certain she'd left it there. She wasted no time looking anywhere else, but turned and ran after the three women and the children. Her heart was filled with a sudden dread.

She arrived at the old hangar and ran in to find the muzzle of her Ingram waiting for her. Lisa Frane held the subgun cocked and ready.

18

Politician dashed after Lyons to meet George Yates and his Libyan terrorists. Able Team's hearts-and-minds expert was trying to look at their tactical situation as Ironman would see it. The situation wasn't pleasant.

About forty terrorists approached in five vehicles. They had opened the convoy into a wide arc, reaching to engulf the cluster of tents. It would be a tricky matter to delay them long enough to give the women and children time to hide. Able Team would be forced into a defensive war—not something to look forward to when outnumbered five to one.

Light autofire was already reaching for the defenders from the approaching four-by-fours. The lightness of the ammunition and the bouncing of the vehicles combined to make the fire less than effective.

Ironman came to a screeching stop and raised his Konzak. He aimed at a truck coming straight for him and squeezed off two careful shots. He then swung his aim and launched another two at a Jeep on his left. The last two were aimed at a station wagon to his right.

Each of the six shots in the clip had held a 350-grain steel ball coated with a layer of lead to give rifling and compression. The result was a .91 ounce ball that left the Konzak with a muzzle speed of four hundred meters per second.

The truck ground to a halt when a steel ball jammed one of its pistons and broke the engine block. The Jeep continued forward spraying oil over the windshield and sand. The station wagon veered away, leaving a trail of oil from a broken block.

Gadgets reached Ironman's side as the Jeep bore directly toward him. The MAC-11 growled, spitting a line of .45 caliber, 230-grain harvesters across the Jeep's windshield.

With three .45 ACP's racing through his skull, the driver's concentration was shot to hell. He let go of the wheel. It spun, and the Jeep flipped, dumping men in an arc around Lyons.

Politician had time to send his regards to the Jeep at the left end of the charging semicircle. His last HE grenade arced perfectly, but arrived too soon. The driver spun the wheel to avoid driving over the grenade. The sharp turn plus the blast knocked the Jeep on its side, but none of the terrorists were hurt.

Quincey had run to the right of Able Team. He found himself facing the truck that had escaped Politician's incendiary grenade at Socorro. Both Ingrams bucked in his huge fists like wild jack rabbits, but he kept the double stream of ACP death notices tearing through the cab and into the back of the truck.

Terrorists leaped from the swaying truck as soon as the firefight began. Those who waited for the truck to slow either jumped a few seconds later or had their legs cut out from under them.

The driver lived through the deadly barrage by sliding off the seat to the floor of the truck. He held the steering wheel in his left hand and held down the accelerator with his right. The engine block absorbed the bullets headed the driver's way. The first two cylinders died, but the other six kept the truck barreling down on Quincey.

One Ingram was empty before Quincey leaped to one side. His timing was slightly off, and the fender brushed him and sent him spinning. He landed hard, losing his wind. Dazed, one gun empty and the other down to a few rounds, Pat Quincey tried focusing his eyes. They didn't coordinate. He saw double. It seemed as if an entire battalion were moving in on him.

Lao Ti sped over the sand, she saw the main body of enemy killers leap from the truck that had knocked Quincey down. It was impossible to reach him before the enemy. When she was still a hundred and fifty yards away, she threw herself on the sand and forced herself to breathe deeply and evenly.

She lined up the caseless on the closest terrorist and caressed the trigger lightly. Her breathing spoiled her aim, and she had to send another brief burst, low and to the left. The startled terrorist dived headfirst into the stream of bullets.

Lao took a deep breath, let part of it out and lined up her sights on another charging present from Khaddafi. This time the burst cored his chest as if it were an apple. She swept her sights along, but the others had gone to ground. She anxiously scanned the rolling surface of the desert with her eyes.

IN THE OLD HANGAR, Karen looked at Frane coldly.

"Yeah," Frane acknowledged, "it's your weapon. I wouldn't try taking it back if I were you."

Karen turned her back on the willowy, younger woman and walked toward the others. The redheaded nurse was berating herself for not having guessed the truth. Of course Lisa was just the type of younger woman George would go for. What made them so susceptible to his influence? Karen wondered.

"Everyone okay?" she asked.

"So far," Dannie answered.

"Sit down," Frane barked. Her voice was hoarse with tension.

"It's better not to antagonize her," Dannie advised Karen. "She's frightened, and frightened people do irrational things."

Karen shrugged and sat down. She was beginning to feel immense pressure. It was her weapon the woman had. As long as the children were hostages, Able Team would be helpless.

It was as if Dannie could see Karen's guilt evolving into raging anger. The psychiatrist put a gentle hand on her arm. "You aren't responsible for the actions of others," Dannie told her. "But you must control your own."

The calm voice steadied Karen. She turned her mind to the problem of getting the weapon away from Frane.

LYONS SAW Gadgets was taking care of the Jeep that was bearing down on him. He turned his concentration to changing clips and doing a quick survey of the war zone.

Able Team had scored a minor victory. The enemy was no longer mobile, although most of them were still very fit for fighting. Unwilling to meet the superior weapons and marksmanship head-to-head, the ninja-trained fighters were trying to corner their prey. They melted into the desert, taking water containers from the vehicles with them.

"Stay low and fall back," Lyons shouted.

It galled him to retreat just when he had the other side also retreating. But he couldn't risk having them cut Able Team off from the children they were trying to defend. Without defensive fortifications, and there were certainly none in the desert, a defensive war was bound to go against the smaller force.

THE TERRORISTS' TALKATIVE COPILOT sat handcuffed to the arm of a seat in the 747-SP. He waited until he was sure that the oriental woman wouldn't suddenly reappear. Then he yanked his arm off the seat. Although the armrests looked like a continuous loop of metal, they had been designed to lift out, if necessary. He slid the plastic cuff off the tubing and put the rest back in place.

First he examined the flight engineer, who was still unconscious but breathing easily. He considered waking and freeing the man, who was cuffed to the frame of a front seat, but rejected the thought. He still didn't trust the flight engineer.

With the cuff loop dangling from his wrist, he moved swiftly toward the flight deck. He paused to make sure he was alone. From under the engineer's seat he removed a Phillips screwdriver. Then he continued to the main cargo hold. In the forward part of the hold, he used the screwdriver on an access hatch, being careful not to let it slip to leave telltale scratches around the screws.

He lifted away the two-foot-square panel and slid his arm far to one side. At first the terrorists' secret weapon cache seemed empty, but extending his arm farther he found them—five new Stechin automatics. They were loaded, but there weren't any spare clips or extra ammunition.

He tucked one automatic in his belt and put another in the left pocket of his pants. He pulled the clips from the remaining three guns and placed them in the other pocket.

He carefully replaced the access cover and then carried the three empty weapons and the screwdriver with him. He stashed the screwdriver behind a seat cushion as he passed through the passenger area. When he reached the open door, he threw the empty handguns to the ground before hustling down the ladder. The sound of autofire was very loud. No one was paying any attention to the crippled plane.

He paused partway down the ladder to take in the scene. From ten feet off the ground he could see glimpses of George Yates's group circling the smaller force that had taken the Boeing. The smaller force was slowly pulling back toward an old aircraft hangar. The copilot had overheard enough conversation on the short flight to guess that a group of children were sheltered in the old building.

He scanned the horizon and sighed. There was no way to walk away from the fight. It was too long a hike through the desert. He had to commit himself to one side or the other and hope he chose the winner.

From his perch he saw George Yates's group making temporary caches of water and ammunition. Water could well be the deciding factor. Those with water had merely to wait until those without were too dehydrated to put up a fight. As long as the smaller group was contained, the result was inevitable.

The American finished climbing down the ladder, then stood in thought for a while. He reached a decision and quickly began to crawl toward the terrorist perimeter.

QUINCEY TOOK A MOMENT to adjust. His enemies were dying in front of him. He rolled onto his back and fed fresh clips into the two subguns.

Patrick Henry Quincey had been a soldier in Vietnam before he was either a minister or a psychotherapist. He knew the enemy's next move. They'd stay low and encircle their prey, then put the squeeze on, depending on their ninja training to eliminate the enemy one at a time.

He was glad he didn't have to general this battle; it looked bad. Brognola was technically in charge of Stony Man, but it was obvious that the head Fed was bowing to Lyons's strategic genius in the battlefield. Quincey wondered what Lyons would do. He couldn't guess. No one could guess what Lyons would do next.

He recognized the slower cyclic rate of Lao's Heckler & Koch G-11. It had the same rate of fire as the enemy's PPSh-41s but made less noise, and the sound was more uniform. With Lao covering his ass, Quincey decided he could begin to move.

He rolled over a small ridge of sand and charged to his left. Two of the terrorists had begun a stealthy withdrawal. They were unprepared for the sudden attack from the man they thought they had pinned. The two subguns spat three-round bursts. One terrorist collapsed as deep red blood sprayed the sand behind him. The second terrorist rolled, and the .45 ACPs bit sand behind him.

Two more fanatics popped up to drill the madman with two guns. One was drilled by Lao instead. The other was so frantic to get his head down again, his shots went wild.

Quincey was about to pursue the other gunman when Lyons shouted to pull back. Throwing himself on his belly, Quincey started the slow backward withdrawal. The enemy would now have a chance to reform and organize.

After taking out the Jeep, Politician worked his way north, trying to contain the enemy and prevent them from end-running to the children. Politician crawled for some minutes without spotting anyone. He put his feet under him and cautiously raised his head.

A bullet snapped by his ear, sending him diving face-down into the scorching white sand. The shot came from someone between Politician and the rest of Able Team. It was time to pull a wide flanking maneuver.

The Able Team warrior began a slow crawl farther away from his teammates in an attempt to move around whoever had cut him off. As he climbed up a slight rise, another bullet snapped over his head. It came from the other side. He was pinned.

After Gadgets took care of his Jeep, he dropped down to reload and then tracked Politician. His friend was in trouble. Gadgets put his feet under him and ran a low zigzag course, taking every possible advantage of the irregularities in the surface of the terrain. Sweat now poured down his body, only to be snatched away by the dry air. Although

Gadgets was well tanned, he knew he was going to have a sunburn, if he lived to enjoy it.

His charge quickly brought him to within sight of the two crawling terrorists. They were scrambling to overtake Politician. Gadgets transferred the MAC-10 to his left fist and pulled the silenced Beretta 93-R from shoulder leather.

The Beretta coughed discreetly. A terrorist plowed six inches of sand with his nose, then stopped. Dead.

Even the slight cough of the Beretta focused attention on Gadgets. The second terrorist rolled onto his back, whipping his PPSh-41 around to bear on Schwarz.

Gadgets didn't take the time for even a look at the rolling target. He dived headfirst behind a slight rise of sand as bullets kicked up small clouds of fine white sand at his heels.

Suddenly the rattle of an M-16 added its voice to the symphony. Gadgets laughed.

"Politician, over here," he called.

Blancanales slid over the dune, lead snatching at the air over his head.

"I was pinned and doubling back to take care of whoever was on my tail when you dealt yourself in. The other one's dead. Thanks."

"Don't talk so much," Gadgets answered. "Let's just bug out."

They began beating their way back to the old hangar as quickly as they could. Their communicators clicked at them. Gadgets kept his on his shoulder where he could reply without holding it. He holstered the Beretta and pushed the transmit button.

"Gadgets and Politician at your service."

"The rest of us are near the hangar. Where are you two?" Lyons voice demanded.

"Coming in from the north. Leave our heads on. We may be bringing uninvited guests."

"Hold the north and northwest quadrants a hundred yards out," Lyons ordered. "You can count on covering fire from the northeast and west."

Gadgets got the picture right away. The Stony Man warriors were holding the hangar, spaced around the perimeter. He and Politician had drawn the territory between the hangar and the 747-SP. He took the northwest quadrant and waved Blancanales to directly in front of the hangar.

The Able Team warrior surveyed his position. It was almost impossible to see from the glaring sand into the deep shadow of the hangar. Pol squinted that way for some time without seeing or hearing movement.

He used his communicator to tell the rest of the team, "Cover the front. It's too quiet in that shed. I'm going in to see what's up."

Politician crawled slowly toward the huge open hangar, but he could still see and hear nothing. He began to make out the motionless faces of the children when he was ten feet from the opening. It wasn't natural for children to sit still without fidgeting. He was so intent on the children that he didn't see Frane until she thrust her hands out, letting the sunlight fall on the MAC-11.

"Let go of your gun, or I'll start shooting," Frane said in a harsh voice.

Politician was stuck. He rose to his knees, leaving the combo weapon in the sand.

"I know you've got a mini-Uzi under your fatigues. Don't put a hand near it."

Politician nodded.

"Now take out your communicator. Slowly!"

Politician moved in slow motion.

"Now raise that blond maniac and tell him he has a choice. Either he surrenders or the children will be hurt.

George wants the children alive. Nothing like kids to make the parents work their asses off for you." She laughed a dry, humorless snort.

19

Politician reached slowly for his communicator. Frane watched him as intently as a cat watches an injured mouse. The Able Team warrior clicked the communicator once, then twice.

"Yeah?" Ironman answered.

"Frane says we should surrender. She has a MAC-11 trained on the youngsters."

There was a pause, then Lyons said, "Sending Quincey to look at the situation. He'll be right in."

"Quincey's on his way," Politician told Frane.

"I heard."

She moved swiftly, placing herself among the children to keep Lyons from firing at her.

Pat Quincey strode in. Both Ingrams were in thigh clips. He held his big hands straight out in front of him as if he were about to catch a ball. Usually his blue eyes reflected calm, but this time they were the blue of superheated steel. They glowed with maniacal intensity.

"Throw down your weapons," Frane demanded. "You, too, Politician. I have children between us. Anything funny, and they go when you go."

Gunfire broke out on the perimeter, but no one inside the old hangar noticed.

Politician began the slow motion movement toward his shoulder harness. It was as if Quincey hadn't heard Frane.

He started striding toward her, shouting in a thunderous voice.

"You'd dare to threaten these children! You say you'll shoot those you cared for and nourished. Are you really that depraved?

"Go ahead. There's Sharon who you nursed through her cold. Put your gun to her head and splatter her brains all over the others. Go ahead! Show us what a worthy person you are."

The small subgun roared, and a three-round burst chewed flesh from Quincey's arm. The big man staggered but didn't fall. He watched, helpless, as Karen tackled Frane from the side.

As Frane was thrown off-balance, Quincey recovered and lashed out with his foot, breaking her right hand and knocking the subgun to the sand.

The firing was particularly heavy on the east side of the hangar, but no one inside paid it much attention.

Dr. Valosky ran to Quincey and started to tear clothing away from around his wound.

Politician pivoted up his mini-Uzi to cover Frane.

"Don't move," he warned her. His usually suave voice couldn't disguise his disgust for her actions.

"Nor you," an amused voice said from just inside the west side of the hangar opening.

George Yates stood in the shadow, grinning. He held a Stechin on the group. His two backups had Russian subguns.

WITH POLITICIAN GONE from the north quadrant and Quincey gone from the west, Gadgets suddenly found himself with a very wide perimeter to cover. Those on the other side of the gaps couldn't help him. They were dealing with a heavy assault from the southeast.

When four more terrorists bore down from the north, Gadgets met them with .45 ACPs, killing two and driving two to ground. It wasn't an easy fight because they didn't come at him in a tight group.

At the height of the gun battle, three figures, using the oriental arts of the ninja, moved past him. The only reason they didn't try to shoot the Stony Man warrior in the back was that they wanted the noise of his gun to cover their entrance to the building. Most of Allah's troops were launching the distraction assault on the other side. They'd make a counterattack the moment they thought the man at their backs had been taken out.

Gadgets, flanked by two determined killers, began a slow, careful retreat, cutting south toward the building. Suddenly he stopped his back crawl and looked at the track he'd just crossed.

Grabbing his communicator, hc rasped, "Someone has penetrated our lines and passed my position."

Lyons's taut voice crackled back, "Hold position. Lao, eliminate infiltrators."

A split second after the brief message, Gadgets heard the Konzak roar on full-auto. It didn't sound as deadly as Lyons's voice had. Schwarz had had years to learn to recognize Lyons's mood from his tone of voice.

Ironman was about to go mad!

There was nothing Gadgets could do about it. He had enemy at his back and enemy in front of him. He couldn't leave his position. Lao was going to find the infiltrators. Gadgets decided he'd better take care of the enemy in front as quickly as possible.

He yanked a grenade from his belt and sent it flying to the last position he'd been shot at from. Then he was on his feet and charging, determined to take advantage of the brief distraction the grenade would cause.

WHEN GEORGE YATES SPOKE, there was absolute silence in the old hangar. Then Quincey rolled over, out of the doctor's hands. A MAC-10 was in his right hand roaring its terrible defiance. The children were well to one side of the line of fire between Quincey and the three terrorists.

Quincey expressed his disgust in 230-grain lead piranhas that chewed the flesh from the two backup gunners. Yates was left unscathed.

Politician smoothly shifted his mini-Uzi from Frane to George Yates and squeezed off a figure eight. Twenty 9 mm avengers ripped through the terrorist leader, who died with his finger squeezing the trigger of his Russian automatic.

The moment Politician's Uzi swung away from Frane, she bent down to pick up the MAC-11 Quincey had kicked from her hand. Karen dived into her, shoving her forward into the spray of Russian lead intended for Quincey.

Dannie Valosky was the first to recover from the sudden blitz of death. She reached over and rolled Quincey back to her so she could tend his wounds. He held on to his weapon, but allowed himself to be rolled.

"Norma! Make sure the children keep flat." Dannie's sharp voice jolted Johnson out of her shock.

Karen gave a gasp and ran to George Yates. She didn't touch him, but stood looking down at his bullet-riddled body.

"He was my husband," she told Blancanales.

But Politician didn't hear her. He had quickly recharged his mini-Uzi and let it swing back under his arm. Then he picked up his over/under combo and examined that. By the time Karen spoke, he had his communicator out and was trying to raise Lyons.

Gadgets's voice came back over the communicator. "Ironman's gone walking."

"Shit!" Politician said, and dashed from the old building.

IT WAS A LONG JOG for the lanky American copilot. The relentless heat from the sun made it twice as difficult. His main fear was that he had started circling the battlefield in the wrong direction. He doubted that he had the endurance to circumnavigate the entire area.

Just when he was beginning to lose hope, he found what he was looking for—the tracks of men to an area farther into the Jornada del Muerto. He followed those tracks away from the battle zone.

Fifty yards farther on, he found a spot where the sand had been scraped away and pushed back. He dug frantically. It took ten minutes of digging with his bare hands to unearth the first water container. He sat back and drank deeply, letting much of the water dribble down his chin and over his once-neat uniform shirt.

Then he cleared sand away from the tops of the other containers. Soon he had them all uncovered. The terrorists had been in a hurry to rejoin their companions and hadn't buried their water supply deeply enough.

After one last drink, the copilot walked around the plastic containers and put a bullet through each. Then he shoved the Stechin back in his belt and picked up two of the dribbling five-gallon jugs. He walked back to the battle zone, leaving a trail of moisture on the sand, a trail that vanished in seconds.

He steered his steps toward the heaviest shooting. Soon he stopped and peered over a small rise. Ahead of him, a half-dozen Libyans were lying on a bank of sand, firing on the defenders. The copilot tossed the two empty containers at them and ran like hell.

He chose a wide circle that would bring him back to the 747-SP. There was nowhere else to go.

IRONMAN HAD HAD ENOUGH.

He'd been taking the brunt of the diversionary assault and could scarcely stick his head up to fire.

The terrorists had called all the shots to date. Able Team had followed them around like a pup, nipping at their heels. The time had come to go for the throat. In a battle of attrition, Able Team didn't stand a chance.

Lyons rammed a twenty-round box of flesh-shredders into his Konzak and stood up. Two bursts of autofire swept toward him immediately. The assault shotgun boomed once, cutting off one sweep of lead before it reached him.

Groaning, Brognola jumped up on Lyons's left to send a burst of 9 mm parabellums from the MAC-11 through the head of another gunner.

Lao was making her way back from the hangar. The situation there was under control, and by the sound of the gunfire she knew that Lyons could still use some help.

It was then that she heard the shouts of anger and despair from the enemy lines. She made out the word *ma*, Arabic for water. Something about water had them extremely upset.

Her glance in that direction caught Ironman as he rose to his feet, firing. She saw Brognola scramble to cover Lyons's left. She sprinted to cover the right.

Two more killers popped up to try their luck at the striding man with the blazing yellow hair. Lao's G-11 sent a burst that went in through the windpipe of one and out through his spine. The other one was too busy diving for cover to bother shooting.

Politician emerged from the shade of the hangar and took in the action at a glance. Lyons was striding after the enemy, his shotgun laying down a heavy pattern of annihilation. From the other direction, Gadgets had succumbed to Lyons's madness. He was tossing grenades and wading into the enemy as if he'd been granted personal immunity from death. Politician sprinted that way to cover Gadgets's back.

Politician's unexpected arrival on Gadgets's tail ruined the plans of three Libyan gunners. The M-16 cancelled their interest in making new plans. They danced for two seconds, then lay down to rest forever. Blancanales slammed home a fresh clip and took off after Gadgets once more.

The loss of their water supply and of their leader at the same time was too much for the fanatical Arabs. Commending their souls to Allah, they all charged in on the hangar, desirous only of killing as many as possible before they themselves died. To their warped minds, Allah didn't care whether the souls sent before them belonged to his enemies or to innocent children.

The charge ended the battle quickly. With superior weapons and coolness under fire, the Stony Man warriors assumed firing-range stances and carefully picked off each enemy they saw. Three minutes later they had run out of targets.

BROGNOLA COMPLETED his slow march around the damaged landing gear of the 747-SP. He stopped when he came to the copilot, who was sitting in the shade of the plane, leaning against a massive tire. The copilot held up a thermos jug, the plastic cuff still dangling from his wrist.

"Coffee?"

Brognola settled down beside him in the sand and shared a drink from the lid of the jug.

"Ironman figures you demolished the water supply and delivered a pair of shot-up containers to them."

The copilot nodded.

"Why?"

The man ignored the question, asking one of his own instead. "What was that helicopter that landed?"

"State police. They'll be sending army air transport for us."

The copilot sighed. "Means jail for me."

"Not necessarily. Why did you help?"

"I'm not sure anyone will understand."

"Try me."

"I have a record. Got caught smuggling a few pounds of Mary Jane into L.A. Did a couple of years. When I got out, this was the only flying job I could get. I knew something stank, but had no idea that we were transporting kill teams. I was afraid to ask any questions.

"But not asking questions has gotten me into worse trouble than smuggling. I decided I had to right the scales somehow. I wanted to feel clean again. Besides, there's something about you people that demands other people around you develop consciences in a hurry. I told you it wouldn't make sense."

Brognola grinned. "What do you think makes these people lay their lives on the line day after day?"

"I guess they have bigger consciences than most people."

"That's one way of putting it. Warriors tend to be very concerned with right action. You know, the government now has a law that allows a law-enforcement agency to seize criminal goods for its own use. It's easy to get the rights to $100,000 worth of criminal property."

"I heard something like that," the pilot replied, puzzled by the change of subject.

"I figure the cost of getting this plane back into the air is going to be immense."

"It's a long way to bring in the jacks and technicians," the copilot agreed.

"I'm going to convince the court that this baby's worth less than $100,000."

"Think you'll make it stick?"

"Terrorists aren't popular. If the choice is between accepting my argument and returning the plane to whoever supplied it to those killers, my argument will stick."

"So?"

"So I'd probably sell it for a small price. Know any potential buyers?"

Just then Ironman strode up to the two of them. "Hey," he shouted, "Quincey and Karen are going to get hitched."

Brognola frowned. "How does Politician feel about that?"

"He'll get over it."

Brognola and the other man stood up.

"How are the kids?" the copilot asked.

Lyons looked at him carefully, reading nothing but genuine concern on the other's face.

"Doc says they're shook up, but in the long run seeing the people who caused their terror destroyed will be beneficial. She's sure they'll all become normally maladjusted teenagers."

"Great," Brognola said. "Maybe we'll find an Able Team recruit among them, someone to take over when this action gets to be too much for an old guy like you, Lyons."

Carl Lyons turned to walk away, and then he laughed.

4 FREE BOOKS
1 FREE GIFT
NO RISK
NO OBLIGATION
NO KIDDING